choker

elizabeth woods

SIMON & SCHUSTER BFYR

New York   London   Toronto   Sydney

SIMON & SCHUSTER BFYR

An imprint of Simon & Schuster Children's Publishing Division
1230 Avenue of the Americas, New York, New York 10020

SIMON & SCHUSTER BFYR is a trademark of
Simon & Schuster, Inc.
For information about special discounts for bulk purchases, please contact Simon &
Schuster Special Sales at 1-866-506-1949 or business@simonandschuster.com.
The Simon & Schuster Speakers Bureau can bring authors to your live event. For
more information or to book an event, contact the Simon & Schuster Speakers
Bureau at 1-866-248-3049 or visit our website at www.simonspeakers.com.

alloy**entertainment**
Produced by Alloy Entertainment
151 West 26th Street, New York, NY 10001

Book design by Andrea C. Uva
The text for this book is set in Sabon.
Manufactured in the United States of America
2 4 6 8 10 9 7 5 3 1
Library of Congress Cataloging-in-Publication Data
Woods, Elizabeth Emma.
Choker / Elizabeth Woods.
p. cm.
Summary: Teenaged Cara, solitary and bullied in high school, is delighted to
reconnect with her childhood best friend Zoe whose support
and friendship help Cara gain self-confidence, even as her classmates start dying.
ISBN 978-1-4424-1233-0 (hardcover)
[1. Best friends—Fiction. 2. Friendship—Fiction. 3. Mental illness—Fiction.
4. High schools—Fiction. 5. Schools—Fiction.] I. Title.
PZ7.W86346Ch 2011
[Fic]—dc22
2010034672
ISBN 978-1-4424-1235-4 (eBook)

FIRST
EDITION

For Jess

"COME OUT, COME OUT, LITTLE FROG. WE'VE MADE YOU a nest. It's under a log." Zoe's clear voice piped through the shaggy thicket of honeysuckle. Nine-year-old Cara stuck a leaf in the little heap of grass and paused to gaze at her best friend.

Zoe sat cross-legged in a little patch of sunlight that filtered through the arching branches overhead. The sun gleamed off her long, blue-black hair, as if reflecting off a pool of water. She must have sensed Cara's eyes because she turned and fixed Cara with her intense violet stare. She smiled. "Maybe tonight a frog will come and sleep in our nest," she said.

Cara nodded and patted the nest she and Zoe had arranged in the woods behind Zoe's house. "Then in the morning, we can creep down here, really quietly, and peek in—"

"And he'll be all curled up, snoring!" Zoe finished, dissolving into laughter. The two girls grinned at each other. Then Zoe's face lit up. "Hey—" She scooted over until her blue-jeaned knee pressed against Cara's. "Do you want to see a secret my mom has in her room?" she whispered. Her breath was hot on Cara's cheek.

Cara's heart beat a little faster. It always did when Zoe got that intense look in her eyes. That look meant something exciting was going to happen. "Won't we get in trouble?" she whispered back.

Zoe's hot, sweaty hand closed around Cara's. "It's okay. No one's home." She pulled Cara to her feet.

The two girls crept out of the honeysuckle. A dog, hearing their movement, barked fiercely on the other side of the high wooden fence. Cara jumped and tripped over a rusty tricycle lying on its side. Broken plastic toys lay strewn everywhere in the small backyard. Tipsy pine trees dripped their branches over the long grass.

Zoe pushed open the rusty screen door and led the way into a little dark hallway. The house smelled of old eggs. Boxes were piled up everywhere. Cara followed her friend up a narrow flight of stairs and into a small front bedroom with windows overlooking the sidewalk.

Zoe tiptoed over to a small, old-fashioned wooden table on one side of the bed. Cara felt nervous excitement bubble in her stomach. She couldn't help giggling. "Won't your mom get mad that we're in her room?" she half-whispered to Zoe as she looked around. The bed was a sea of rumpled sheets and blankets. Clothes were draped over the back of an easy chair and strewn on the carpet, as if someone had left in a hurry. Through the smeary glass, Cara could just make out the neat white shutters of her own house across the street.

Zoe didn't answer. Cara heard the scrape of wood and turned around to see her wrestling with a little drawer in the table. "Wait, I'll help you," Cara said, putting her hand over Zoe's on the wooden knob. Together they pulled one more time. The drawer screeched open.

"Got it!" Zoe stuck her hand in the drawer and pulled out a small orange bottle of pills. She held it up triumphantly. Cara's eyes widened. "They're like zombie pills," Zoe said. "They make you reeaallly spaaccey." She held her arms out in front of her, the bottle still clutched in one hand, and staggered around the room with her eyes closed, bumping into the dresser. "Ow." She giggled, opening her eyes. "Want to see?" Zoe extended the bottle toward Cara.

Gingerly, Cara accepted the small orange bottle. Just holding it felt deliciously scary. She rotated the bottle around until she could see the label, but it was full of long medicine words ending in "-zol" and "-zone." The only part she could understand read *Take one (1) per day with food. Do not miss a dose. Doing so could cause recurrence of symptoms.*

Zoe grabbed the pills out of Cara's hand and started dancing around the room. "Zommmbie pills!" she shouted, jumping on the unmade bed. She shook the bottle over her head.

"Zommbies!" Cara shouted too, and jumped on the bed alongside her friend. The two of them collapsed on the sheets in hysterical laughter. Cara rolled onto her back and looked over. Zoe's eyes were fixed on her.

"What is it?" Cara asked.

A little smile flickered across Zoe's face. She sat up and with one swift movement, twisted off the white bottle cap and dumped the pills out in front of her.

Cara sat up, too. They both stared at the heap of shiny blue capsules as if waiting for them to come to life. Zoe reached

3

out and stirred them around. "Try one," she said suddenly.

"What?"

Zoe pinched one of the capsules between her thumb and forefinger. "Try one. Just to see what it's like." She was smiling, but her voice was low and intense. She held out the little blue pill.

Cara shook her head. "No, thanks. I don't really feel like turning into a zommbie right now." She rolled her eyes around, hoping her friend would laugh.

But Zoe continued holding out the pill. "Come on. Don't be a baby." She edged closer to Cara. Their faces were almost touching.

"I'm not," Cara said weakly.

"Then take it."

Zoe's violet eyes seemed to be pinning Cara against the headboard of the bed. The air in the room was thick and unmoving. Cara could feel a trickle of sweat running down the side of her face.

Then suddenly Zoe sat back. She tossed her long hair over her shoulder. "It's okay, Car." She smiled gently. "*I'm* not scared. I'll just take one first. Then you'll see it's not a big deal." She slowly brought her fingers toward her mouth.

"Cara!" The voice came faintly from the outside.

Both girls jumped. Zoe dropped the pill she was holding. It tumbled off the bed and rolled into a dusty corner. Cara scrambled off the bed and rushed to the window. Her mother was standing on the sidewalk below, a trench coat thrown over her T-shirt, looking around anxiously. "Cara!" she called again.

Cara spun around. Zoe was perched at the edge of the

bed, her hands in her lap. She had returned the pills to the bottle. It now sat innocently on the bedside table.

"I guess I have to go," Cara said.

"Guess so." Zoe got up and walked with her out of the room and down the narrow stairs.

In the hall, Cara pushed the screen door open. "See you tomorrow?"

Zoe shrugged. "I don't know. I might have stuff to do." Her face was bland.

"But what about the frog nest?" Cara stammered.

Zoe studied her for a second. Then she smiled. "Oh, yeah. I forgot. Want to come over in the morning?"

Cara nodded. Zoe reached out and hugged her tightly.

"See you tomorrow," Cara called as she clattered down the porch stairs.

"Tomorrow," she heard Zoe echo faintly.

Chapter 1

CARA LANGE STOOD IN THE DOORWAY OF THE CAFE-
teria, her nylon lunch bag in one hand. The din of
chattering students floated above the sea of white
Formica-topped tables, and a steamy potato-and-onion aroma
emanated from the kitchen. Cara paused. She wasn't sure she
could stand another lunch tacked onto the other track girls
like a vestigial organ—completely useless and unnecessary.
She considered fleeing to the parking lot and eating lunch in
her yellow '99 Volvo. But no. She wasn't that lame.

Not yet.

Cara forced her legs across the brown-tiled room. Sherman
High hadn't done a lot of updating since its construction in
1975, architecture's notorious Brutalism phase. People driving
by often mistook the sprawling building on the outskirts of Des
Moines for a prison. Cara could have told them that assump-
tion wasn't far from the truth.

She passed the emo kids in the corner, and the hipsters with
their retro T-shirts, and the hippies eating organic yogurt.
Some of the art students were stacking a bunch of chairs into

a tower—some kind of new art installation? The track girls were clustered at their usual table, packed in tightly. Sarit Kohli, her dark braid reaching almost to her waist, inhaled a stack of turkey slices as she told Rachael Meade about yesterday's practice. Julie Cohen chomped loudly on an apple while laughing at something Madeline Brazelton was texting. Cara stood over them for a minute, smiling vaguely, but no one looked up or even stopped talking. Finally, she dragged a chair over from the next table and squeezed in between Sarit and Madeline.

"Oh, hey, Cara," Sarit said, looking up. She inched her chair over.

"Thanks." Cara sat down.

"Sure." Sarit shrugged, already turning back to Rachael.

Cara let the noise of the room swirl around her like smoke as she pulled a bag of baby carrots from her nylon sack and nibbled idly. Her eyes drifted across the room to the cafeteria door. Prom-princess Alexis Henning was just swaying through the doors, her butter-blond hair spilling in perfect waves over her shoulders. By her side was Ethan Gray, her on-again, off-again boyfriend and the captain of the boys' track team. Alexis's beefy-faced best friend—and Cara's next-door neighbor—Sydney Powers scurried by her side. Cara's shoulders tightened involuntarily.

The group slouched into chairs at their usual table nearby. For the gazillionth time, Cara studied Ethan's profile, taking in the icy-blue eyes, gorgeous nose, and perfectly scruffy beard stubble. His thick dark hair just brushed the collar of his navy polo. Cara sat back in her chair and mentally ran her fingers over his chiseled cheeks.

"*You forgot to shave,*" she pictured herself teasing. "*I don't want to get all scratched up when you kiss me.*"

"*Too bad,*" she heard him say. He leaned over her and pulled her up against him. She could feel the hard muscles of his chest. He bent his head toward hers. She closed her eyes. . . .

Alexis's screechy voice crowded her ear. "You can't come to Sydney's tomorrow, Ethan. It's girls only, you dork."

Cara opened her eyes. Three tables over, Alexis was pulling the foil top off a Dannon lemon yogurt using only the tips of her fingers. Ethan leaned over and whispered something in her ear. "Eww, you're disgusting!" She slapped him on the shoulder, and he grinned.

Cara took a deep breath. Her fingers were squeezing a baby carrot, and she forced them to relax. Sydney's surprisingly deep voice chimed in. "My next party is going to be all boys, Ethan—and us, of course."

Cara resisted the urge to bury her face in her hands. Sydney's house was practically on top of her own. Which meant that every Friday and Saturday night, Cara sat at home, alone, pretending to watch *Real Housewives* on TiVo while trying to ignore the squeals and laughter from Sydney's deck.

God, if only Zoe were here. A familiar twist of pain tightened Cara's abdomen at the thought of her old best friend. She hadn't seen Zoe since her family moved away in fifth grade. It was like her other half was missing.

Cara pushed her lunch aside and pulled a notebook from her bag. She doodled idly in the margins. She hadn't thought about Zoe in a while, but recently, for some reason, her mind was filled with memories of her. The two of them climbing the wild grapevines in the woods behind Zoe's house, pretending to be forest princesses. Trying to tame the neighbor's crazy German shepherd with pieces of cupcake, then screaming when he barked. All the times Zoe had snuck into her bedroom at night through the window, crying because of her horrible stepdad. She'd climb under the comforter and Cara would stroke her silky dark hair until Zoe fell asleep.

They'd written to each other some after the move, but pretty soon the letters just stopped. Cara had a feeling her parents were relieved to have Zoe gone. They used to act so weird whenever Cara brought up her friend; it was like they thought Zoe and her family weren't good enough. Not that they were really in a position to decide what was good for Cara. She'd been stuck with one babysitter after another until she was old enough to stay alone, all so Mom and Dad wouldn't miss a single moment in the courtroom.

Cara looked down at her notebook. Without even realizing it, she'd drawn little pictures of her and Zoe all up and down the margins. She glanced around hurriedly, but no one had noticed. Sarit was staring fixedly at her phone, while Julie leaned over her shoulder, pointing out something on the screen. The others were cramming the rest of their lunches into their mouths. It was only a few minutes until the next bell. Quickly, Cara ripped out the page and stuffed it in the back pocket of her frayed navy chinos.

Just then, a girl's shrill laugh rose above the rest of the noise in the cafeteria. Cara looked up. Across the room, Jack Penn slung Alexis up over his meaty shoulder, fireman-style.

"Stop it, Jack!" she screeched delightedly, pounding on his back with her manicured hands. He twirled her faster, and everyone at Cara's table snickered. Finally Jack set Alexis on her feet. Then he leaned over and whispered something in her ear. She laughed like a donkey, showing all her teeth.

Cara kept her eyes fixed on Ethan as he sat across the table, his brow darkening. She couldn't believe Alexis would flirt with Jack so obviously right in front of him. Ethan rose to his feet and leaned over, his palms on the table, as he said something to Alexis. Cara watched intently as they argued back and forth, Alexis's arms crossed over her chest, Ethan scowling. She couldn't hear what they were saying, but it didn't take a neuroscientist to figure it out. He turned away as if to leave. Cara gripped the edge of the table so hard her fingertips turned white. But Alexis caught Ethan's hand and pulled him toward her.

Cara closed her eyes for a long moment. When she opened them, Alexis and Ethan were locked in a passionate kiss, his arms around her waist, hers clutching his neck.

Cara slumped back in her chair. Of course. Same old story.

Ethan and Alexis got up and wove their way through the packed lunchroom toward the door. Ethan stopped every few feet to talk to people. Cara watched him high-five Ms. Sitwell, the school secretary, then sighed and stood up. She might as well get a head start on her calc homework. She folded her foil into a square and stuffed it back in her nylon sack, then nodded good-bye to the rest of the table. Sarit gave her a little wave, but the others didn't even look up.

Stuffing the last bite of baby carrot into her mouth, Cara pushed in her chair. But one of the legs stuck, and Cara lurched a little against the table edge. She felt a chunk of unchewed carrot slide down the back of her tongue and lodge in her windpipe.

11

Automatically, Cara opened her mouth to cough. But no air came through. She leaned over and tried to cough again. Still nothing. Panic rising through her chest, she grabbed at her throat, clawing helplessly at her skin. She looked around wildly. No one had even noticed. They were all clustered around Julie, who was showing them some homework in a binder.

Her lungs were sending distress signals through her body. She could feel her chest tightening. Her eyes bulging, she waved her hands. *Choking, I'm choking,* she tried to telegraph. She tried to retch, but she felt the carrot lodge even more firmly in her throat. The noise around her swirled in a colorful chaos.

I'm dying, and no one's going to notice.

She heard Sarit's voice as if from a great distance. "Cara? Are you okay?"

She shook her head blindly, her hands at her throat. Julie's voice rose. "Oh my God, Cara, what's the matter?"

"She's, like, turning blue!"

"Where? What's the matter?"

A sea of faces danced in front of her. Then Cara felt a pair of arms like steel rods grab her around the middle. Two clasped fists slammed into her diaphragm, once and then twice. The carrot shot up over the back of her tongue and out of her open mouth. Cara watched it roll under the rack of dirty trays like a little orange pinball.

She coughed, a big, gaping open-mouthed hack. A string of drool hung down from her lip. She swiped at it and wheeled around, her face bright red and her eyes watering.

Ethan stood just behind her, his face creased with concern. "Are you okay?" he asked.

12

She nodded, staggering a little, and almost lost her balance. He caught at her arm, and a shock ran through her body at his touch. She coughed again. Her throat felt like it had been doused in battery acid. "Yeah," she gasped. She swiped at her mouth, which was embarrassingly wet. "I'm okay." Her voice came out gravelly. She caught sight of Alexis and Sydney staring at her behind Ethan's shoulder. Alexis's eyes were narrowed.

"Wow, good. That was scary." Ethan released her arm. Cara nodded dumbly and looked around. After sending her a few big-eyed stares, the rest of the girls started drifting away. Her nose was running. She looked around for a tissue. She couldn't stand here in front of Ethan Gray, after he had just saved her life, with a runny nose like a five-year-old. Cara spotted a napkin on the table and snatched it up. She pressed it to her nose as Ethan patted her shoulder. "Cool, glad you're okay." He brushed past her.

"Hey, um, thank—," Cara started to say. But he was already heading back toward the door. Someone smelling of watermelon body spray brushed past her, uncomfortably close. "It's amazing what some people will do for attention, isn't it?" Alexis said loudly to Sydney.

"I know!" Sydney shot a meaningful glance at Cara, then paused, a little smile playing at the corners of her mouth. "Nice one, Choker."

And then they glided away, leaving Cara alone, clutching her damp napkin, her chair overturned at her feet.

Chapter 2

CARA SAW THE FLASH OF MOVEMENT AGAIN DURING MR. Crawford's English class. All day, she'd been seeing it—a faint impression of *something* just inside her peripheral vision. This time it had been by the maple trees. Cara squinted out the half-opened window, brushing back a strand of lank brown hair.

Nothing. Just battered lawn and crystal-blue autumn sky. Flagpole clanking. Fall breeze smelling of leaves wafting past her face. Cedric the janitor wheeling out some trash cans, his blue uniform shirt fluttering on his thin frame. Maybe she should have her eyes checked.

Cara resisted the temptation to lay her head on the scarred wood-veneer desk. Even after tea with honey last night and a Halls drop, her throat still felt shredded. As she entered the lobby this morning, some jerk had called out, "Good morning, Choker!" and a little giggle had rippled through the groups standing around. She heard it again on her way to homeroom— someone murmured "It's Choker" as she brushed through the crowded hallways. Cara fixed her eyes straight ahead and concentrated on maintaining her neutral look. Nonchalance was exhausting.

She let her gaze travel around the sunny room. The discussion of *Catcher in the Rye* buzzed around her like static. Ten people were texting with their phones under their desks, four were reading for other classes, and two were sleeping. Dale Simmons was actually drooling a little. Up at the front of the room, Mr. Crawford tapped his marker on the whiteboard. "Think, folks. Who does Holden Caulfield truly admire? Dale, wake up." Dale's head jerked up. Mr. Crawford scanned the room. "Anybody? Alexis?"

One aisle over, Alexis slid her phone into her bag with a smooth flick of her wrist and offered Mr. Crawford a brilliant smile. A little silver butterfly clip gleamed in her blond hair. "Well, his little sister, right?"

"Right, very good." Mr. Crawford wrote "Phoebe" on the board. Alexis sat back in her chair in a self-satisfied manner and crossed her tanned legs. She reached into her gigantic bag and took out a tube of lip gloss, running it over her mouth until her lips had achieved a sticky purple gleam. Cara could smell the sugary fake grape scent all the way across the aisle. Alexis glanced coolly around the room. Cara looked away, but not fast enough. Alexis leaned over. "What are you looking at?" she hissed, her voice piercing like a shard of ice. "Don't you know it's rude to stare?"

Cara's toes curled inside her battered running shoes. She felt the little muscle at the corner of her eye begin to twitch. Alexis saw it too. She opened her mouth to say something else, but just then, Mr. Crawford turned around. Alexis faced forward fast. Cara exhaled quietly and put her finger over the twitching muscle. She forced herself to take a deep breath and relax until the twitching stopped.

One row over and four up, Ethan stretched his muscular arms behind his head. Just yesterday, those arms were wrapped around her midsection. Cara let her fingers skate along the sore place over her ribs. What if the choking hadn't happened in front of a million people? What if they'd been alone? Maybe he would have helped her to a chair and sat down with her, clasping one of her hands—

"—breakdown, Cara?"

"Huh?" She jumped, banging her knees on the underside of the desk. Her binder clattered to the floor, scattering a handful of papers across the aisles.

The class tittered, and a few people twisted around in their seats to look. Mr. Crawford stroked his scraggly beard patiently. "In your opinion, did Holden's 'phony' parents contribute in some way to his breakdown?" His twinkly little eyes bore down on her from behind his glasses.

Cara could feel her face grow hot. She could sense the class listening. "Um, uh, well, yes?" she mumbled.

"Um, uh, well, *harr-acch*." Alexis made a disgusting retching sound, just loud enough for everyone around them to hear. Next to her, Sydney snorted, and the laughter swelled. Cara's ears flamed. She looked up at Mr. Crawford, hoping he would move on to someone else, but he just offered a sympathetic smile.

"Would you like to refer to your book, Cara?" he asked.

No. No, I most certainly would not like to refer to my book. But thanks for asking. Cara bent her head and riffled through the crumbly yellowed pages in a white heat of embarrassment.

17

The black letters swam together in front of her eyes. For an eternity, the room was silent save for the thud of her heart and Alexis and Sydney's breathy snickers. Finally, she looked up at Mr. Crawford helplessly.

He nodded a little. "Anyone else?" he asked, his eyes sweeping the rest of the class. "Thoughts on Holden's parents?"

Cara went limp. She leaned down and swept up a handful of her fallen papers, then slid down in her chair. Crossing her arms over her old green T-shirt, she stared fixedly at the maples outside. Just then, she saw it—the flash of movement in the trees. It looked like something . . . *someone*, darting behind one of the thick tree trunks. Cara blinked. The flash was gone.

The bell rang. Mr. Crawford raised his voice. "Chapters twelve through sixteen for Wednesday, everyone." There was a general clattering and scraping of chairs. Cara slowly closed her binder. She wanted to make sure Alexis and Co. were out of the hallway before she left. As people filed past, she rummaged around in her messenger bag, pretending she was searching for something in the front pocket.

Someone stopped by her chair. Cara's heart sank. If Alexis said one more thing, she might just break in two. Gingerly, she lifted her eyes an inch. She saw a large pair of boat shoes, one with a broken, knotted lace, and two masculine ankles. She looked up.

Ethan stood in front of her, holding out the rest of her escaped papers. "Hey, these were under my chair," he said. Cara thought she was going to pass out just from the sound of his mellow baritone. His blue eyes seemed to pin her against the chair.

"Th—" Her throat closed up halfway through the word. *Oh my God, Cara, can't you even say "thanks" without looking like an idiot?* She cleared her throat. "Thanks." She stood up too fast, catching her thighs under the desk rim and almost knocking it over.

"Whoa." Ethan reached out to steady the wobbling desk. "Hey, just wanted to see how your throat was feeling. You know, after yesterday."

Cara flushed. "I'm okay," she said in a low voice. She took the papers and held them awkwardly in both hands.

"Cool, that's good. I thought I was going to break your ribs." Ethan grinned. He paused. Cara stood frozen. *Say something! This guy saved your life yesterday!* But all she could produce was a stupid little smile and a shrug. Ethan waited a second longer, fiddling idly with a leather band around his wrist.

"See you at practice." He smiled at her and proceeded up the aisle. She watched him give Alexis a squeeze, then disappear into the hallway.

Cara stuffed the notes into her backpack and yanked the zipper closed, ignoring the wad of paper still sticking out of the side. With her head down, she trudged up the aisle and nodded good-bye to Mr. Crawford. As she rounded the corner into the hallway, someone bumped her hard from behind, almost sending her sprawling onto the battered linoleum floor.

Alexis and Sydney stood there, toothy grins spread across their faces. "Hey, it's Choker!" Alexis declared for the whole hallway to hear. "How's it going today—*arrgh! Haach!*" She clutched her neck as horrible retching sounds issued from her mouth.

"Hooach! Rrack!" Sydney joined in, opening her thick lips so wide Cara could see the fillings in her back teeth. She bulged her eyes out and rolled them around in her head, as if she were about to expire right there in the English wing.

Cara felt her pulse pound in her temples. She whipped around and began walking away, fast. Keeping her eyes straight ahead, she zigzagged between people hurrying to class. Alexis and Sydney followed, making choking noises, every so often dissolving into giggles. "Cara! Cara! Wait!" Alexis called as she neared the lobby.

Cara stopped and turned around. "W-what?" She tried to sound bored, but it came out shaky.

A couple of sophomores stapling swim meet fliers to a bulletin board turned around. Some hairy stoners hurrying out to their cars to smoke actually stopped and watched.

Alexis's eyes gleamed. *"Ooooohhhaack!"* She went into another paroxysm, her biggest so far. Hands at her throat, she twirled around in the middle of the lobby like a manic ballerina.

Cara willed herself to turn around again and keep walking, but her feet wouldn't move. Her stomach was twisted in a painful knot. A crowed gathered around them.

Alexis stopped twirling. "It was really disgusting watching you snot all over yourself," she told Cara conversationally. Cara felt tears gather in the corners of her eyes. Alexis peered at her. "Aw, Cara's upset." She took a tissue from her pocket. "I'm sorry, Cara," she purred. "Here—don't snot on yourself again." She waved the tissue in Cara's face.

"Get away from me!" Cara barked, knocking Alexis's hand away. Her voice rang out in the now-still lobby. A little ripple of laughter went through the crowd. A few kids craned their necks for a better view.

Alexis offered a pearly white smile. "You know, Choker—oops, I mean, Cara—if you'd just chew your food like a normal person, we wouldn't have to see you hark it up. I think that carrot is still there on the floor. Why don't you clean up after yourself, Choker?"

Cara could feel the corner of her eye start twitching again. She could hardly see Alexis's smooth, porcelain face in front of her. All of a sudden, her eyes were swimming with hot tears. She opened her mouth to say something—anything—but no words came out.

Alexis's green eyes narrowed. She bent toward Cara's face. "What's the matter with your eye, Choker?" she asked loudly. "It's, like, jumping around like a spider." She pointed as if noting an interesting medical phenomenon.

A murmur went through the onlookers. "Where?"

"What's her eye doing?"

"Move, I can't see."

People clustered closer. Cara looked around wildly. She could feel the twitching getting faster. She clapped one hand over her eye and, spinning around, shoved her way through the crowd.

She ran down the hallway, the laughter behind her echoing in her ears. The gray bathroom door loomed ahead. Cara shoved it open without slowing down. She bolted into one of the dented metal stalls, leaned over the toilet, and puked.

Gasping, Cara straightened up and slowly wiped her mouth with some toilet paper. At the sink, she buried her hands in slimy pink soap as she stared at her reflection in the mirror. The harsh fluorescent lights cut dark circles under her eyes, which were sunken like pits in her head. The edges of her nostrils were pink-rimmed, and her brown hair hung in limp strands to her shoulders.

Cara shuddered. Slowly, she slid her back down the tiled wall until she was sitting on the floor. The bathroom was utterly silent except for an echo-y *tink-tink* drip of water from one of the faucets. She tilted her head back against the wall and drew her knees against her chest. She closed her eyes and went to a quiet place in her head.

Chapter 3

CARA'S HEAD WAS POUNDING BY THE TIME SHE FINALLY got home at seven o'clock. Practice had been brutal, and now all she wanted was a hot shower and a giant carton of Ben & Jerry's. "Hi," she called as she opened the front door. There was no answer. The spacious foyer was dim and shadowy, the house chilly from being closed up all day.

On the hall chair, her mother's tabby cat, Samson, was curled up on her favorite fleece jacket. "Move, Samson." Cara swatted at him. He rose slowly and gave her a bored feline stare. "Ick." She yanked the jacket out from under him and wiped at the gray hairs stuck all over it. He ignored her and licked his belly.

A pile of mail lay scattered across the floor near the mail slot. Cara switched on the hall lamp and dumped the mail in the already heaping basket on the foyer table. The rest of the table was cluttered with a random collection of sunglasses, bowls of change, and a pile of Christmas cards from nine months ago, coated with a thick layer of dust.

"Mom?" Cara called, wandering into the kitchen. The last of the evening light was filtering through the windows, illuminating the dirty dishes on the counter as if in a still life. Days of newspapers and law journals were heaped on the marble countertops. There was a note taped to the table.

Car—Late meeting. Stew in Crock-Pot. Love you! Mom

She lifted the lid of the Crock-Pot on the counter and gazed at the raw meat and vegetables inside. Mom had forgotten to turn it on again. Cara was hardly surprised; her parents were both attorneys and had always worked long hours, even when she was little. She'd spent most of her childhood with a babysitter or a nanny. There had been a time, though, when they'd first moved here after fifth grade, when they really felt like a family. She always thought of it as the "good period." They went grocery shopping together; they took day trips on the weekends; there was actual conversation at the dinner table. And then as Cara finished middle school, her parents started working more and more, and like a spell wearing off, the "good period" slowly came to an end. Now they were up to seventy-plus hours a week again, just like when she was little.

She was used to the silent house, though, and tonight at least, it was a relief not to have to talk to anyone. It was so quiet, she could hear the furnace click on and off. She slung her bag onto one of the antique ladder-back chairs and collapsed at the table. She let her forearms rest on her sweat-sticky thighs and her hands dangle between her legs. Her head throbbed.

Cara raised her head at the sound of a key at the front door. She heard rustling and the tap of high heels. Her mother breezed in, Burberry trench draped over one arm, her gray hair swept into a disheveled bun. A pair of reading glasses was pushed onto the top of her head, and there were dark circles under her eyes. She set her bulging alligator briefcase on the floor near the doorway and jumped when she saw her daughter sitting in the half-shadows at the table. "Oh! Cara, I didn't realize you were home."

"I thought you weren't going to be back until later." Cara heaved herself up from the table and went over to the fridge. She opened the door, letting the chilly white light bathe her face.

"I actually made it out of court early, can you believe that?" Her mother brushed a strand of hair away from her forehead. "Judge Haney was about to keep us, but then the opposing counsel's client didn't show, so I told him—" She broke off as Samson came mewing into the room, twining himself around her ankles. "Hi, baby!" she cooed. She scooped the cat into her arms and kissed him on the nose.

Cara closed her eyes. When she opened them, her mother was setting a dish of Fancy Feast on the floor. Samson crouched over it, smacking as he ate, while Mom crouched beside him, stroking his back and crooning. Her face wore a tender smile. Cara quietly began edging toward the door. Maybe she could just slip up to her room. Just close the door and—

"Cara!" Her mom looked up. "Where are you going?" She rose from the floor and looked more carefully at her daughter's face. "Honey, you're pale. Did you have a hard day?" She brushed her fingers over Cara's forehead.

Cara jerked away from the irritating softness of her mother's touch. "I'm fine." She kept her voice steady and dug a Diet Coke out of the fridge. "Practice was just a little rough." She forced herself to look at her mother full on, willing her face to betray nothing. She focused on the fine web of wrinkles fanning out from her mother's eyes. Her parents were so much older than anyone else's—sixty and sixty-two. By the time they'd gotten around to having kids, there was only time for one, her mom always said with a laugh.

"Maybe track is too much for you." Her mom's brows knit. "You know Dad and I wanted you to take things easy this year—"

"I'm fine," Cara snapped, her voice rising. She caught herself and inhaled deeply. "I'm fine," she repeated, this time more calmly. "Really. Track isn't that hard. I like it."

"Oh." Her mother dropped her hand. She looked like she wanted to say something more but instead went over to the Crock-Pot and lifted the lid. "Well, I'm glad I made this stew. You need a good dinner."

"It's raw." Cara poured the soda down her throat. "You forgot to turn it on." She knew she was being a brat. But she really wasn't in the mood for her mom's June Cleaver act.

"Oh!" Her mother lifted the lid of the Crock-Pot and stared inside. "Well . . ." She looked around. "How about eggs on toast?"

The old standby. Cara stuck her hand in the cupboard and silently handed her mother the bread.

The front door opened again. A moment later, her father's slender figure appeared in the doorway, his habitual bow tie askew. He was muttering to himself, as usual.

"Hi, Dad."

His distracted gaze cleared a little as he focused on Cara standing near the stove. "Oh. Hi, honey." He wandered over to the fridge. "Get out of court early, Marge?" He took a bottle of Sam Adams out of the fridge.

Mom ripped open a bag of salad greens and dumped them into a bowl, which she set on the table. "Yes, I was just telling Cara that the opposing counsel . . ." She rambled on while her father listened attentively, nodding his head.

The toaster dinged. Mom raked the toast out onto a plate with a fork. "Isn't this nice?" she said. "All of us eating together. We don't do this enough."

Cara sighed. She pulled out the chair at her place and slid a fried egg off the platter onto her toast. With difficulty, she stuck her fork through the overcooked yolk.

They all chewed. Silence filled the kitchen, save for the crunching of toast. Her father's gaze was focused on the wall in front of him. His lips moved a little, and she caught him muttering "motion to dismiss." He'd always been preoccupied with the law, but ever since they moved a few years ago, the cloud of facts and arcane cases that surrounded him had only deepened.

"So, tell us about your day, honey." Mom made another attempt.

Cara forced a pleasant smile. "It was fine." She moved some blackened toast crumbs around on her plate. *Fine*. The only word necessary when speaking to parents.

"That's not very descriptive." Mom laughed a little. Her father was digging around in his salad, searching for the olives.

Cara maintained the pleasant smile. The taste of vomit still filled her mouth. "It was great, Mom. We're reading *Catcher in the Rye* in English."

"I loved that book. Your father did too, didn't you, Don?"

Her dad looked up. "Oh. Yes, marvelous." He returned to his salad. Her mother sat back in her chair tiredly. The kitchen clock's tick was deafening.

After forcing one more bite, Cara laid down her fork with exquisite care. "Thanks for dinner, Mom. I have so much homework, I'm going to get started." She laid her napkin next to her plate and rose from her seat.

"Dad and I are going out for a little bit. A dessert reception at the Waterfront. We'll be back around eleven."

Cara nodded. She took a carton of Phish Food from the freezer, pried the lid off, and dumped in half a bag of raisins and some Cheerios, along with a splash of milk. Grabbing a spoon, she made for the door.

"I'm glad we got a chance to talk, honey!" her mother called, pushing back her chair.

They began stacking the dishes in the sink as Cara climbed the stairs. She didn't bother turning on the lights. She desperately needed a shower. Her track shorts seemed glued to her butt, and even after the egg and toast, the taste of vomit still lingered.

In the long upstairs hallway, she took a big spoonful of her special concoction and set the carton on the hall table, then flicked on the light in the guest bathroom. She deserved the rainfall showerhead in here today, instead of the drippy one in her own bathroom. Cheerful yellow light flooded the little room like an antidote to the shadows in the rest of the house. Downstairs, she could hear keys jingling and her parents talking. Then the front door closed and the house was quiet.

Cara shut the bathroom door firmly and turned the

shower on steaming hot. With a deep sigh, she stripped off her sweaty running clothes and climbed under the pounding spray, letting the water run over the top of her head and down her back. The lemony scent of the citrus body wash seemed to lift her headache right out of her skull.

Cara scrubbed herself all over and shampooed her hair twice. Just as she was rinsing for the second time, she heard a sound in the hallway. She lifted her head, every horror movie she'd ever seen flashing through her mind. For a long moment, she stood tense, sponge still clutched in one hand, ears straining for the sound again. Nothing.

She tilted her head under the water once more. Then she heard it again—a soft rustle and then a thump, right outside the door. Her heart leaped into her throat. Reaching behind her, she carefully shut off the water. Her hand trembled a little as she reached out and pulled her towel from the rack, wrapping it around her streaming body.

The sound came again. *Rustle, thump.*

Cara stared wide-eyed at the door, still firmly shut. Suddenly, she took one giant step out of the tub and swung the door open fast.

Samson crouched on the hall table, his furry head deep in the ice cream container, lapping it up as fast as he could. The container pushed back and forth, the spoon clanking against the wall. *Rustle, thump.*

Cara sagged against the wall, her knees aching with unused adrenaline. Samson glanced up at her. "Get off of there." She swatted at him, and he jumped gracefully off the table, disappearing into her parents' room. Cara shook her head to clear it. She really had to get a grip.

Tightening the towel around her chest and under her arms, Cara padded toward her room at the end of the hall. The walls were shrouded in darkness. She stumbled over a pair of shoes left on the floor and opened the door to her room.

"Hi, Cara."

She screamed and hit the light switch.

Zoe was sitting on her bed, her violet eyes shining.

Chapter 4

CARA STARED AT HER OLD FRIEND, FROZEN. SHE FELT like she was in a dream, unable to speak or move, rooted to the floor.

Zoe just sat there on the edge of Cara's striped bedspread, her bare feet resting on the floor. She wore a dirt-stained navy T-shirt with a pair of jeans ripped at the knee, her hair hanging like a shiny black sheet down her back. Her hands were clasped neatly together in her lap. She stared at Cara, her eyes sparkling, her mouth pursed a little, as if containing a laugh.

"What are you doing here?" Cara finally managed to whisper. Her face felt numb.

"Nice to see you, too!" Zoe rose from the bed, moving with the kind of sinuous grace Cara remembered from their childhood. She was taller, more slender than she'd been seven years ago. Her cheekbones were elegantly prominent. She came close, and Cara could smell cinnamon on her breath. "I thought you'd be glad to see me at least." She stroked Cara's cheek softly. "I've missed you so much."

With the touch of Zoe's hand, Cara woke from her trance.

Her face broke into a grin. She grabbed Zoe up in a hug. "Oh my God, I'm sorry! Of course I'm glad to see you! I was just surprised, that's all." Cara squeezed Zoe's shoulders. "Wow, you're skinny. I can feel your bones."

A rueful little smile twisted Zoe's lips. "Yeah. Things have been rough at home. I fixed everything, though." Together, the girls sank down onto Cara's bed.

Cara took Zoe's hands in hers. "What do you mean, you fixed everything? What's going on? Tell me." She stared intently into her friend's eyes. They were the same, despite the hollows under them. Still those endless pools of amethyst.

Zoe swallowed and looked down at their clasped hands. "Car—it's my stepdad." Her voice was so low, Cara had to bend forward to hear her.

"Oh my God, still? What a bastard." Though she'd never met Zoe's stepdad, Cara felt like she knew him perfectly from her friend's descriptions over the years. His straight, dark hair and big, raw-knuckled hands.

Zoe sniffled a little and wiped the back of her hand under her nose. "He's been coming into my room again . . . just like he used to . . . and . . ." She looked up. Her eyes were huge, magnified by brimming tears. "I ran away. I couldn't think of anywhere else to go."

"I'm so glad you did!" Cara wrapped her arms around her friend's shoulders. "How did you get here?"

"I hitchhiked. It took awhile, getting a ride on the interstate. But this trucker picked me up. He was pretty awful, too—" She shook her head as if to rid herself of the memory. She looked intently into Cara's face. "Listen, Car, I have a huge favor to ask. Can I stay here for a few days? Just until

I figure something out? Please?" Her eyes were pleading. "I saw a newspaper at the truck stop, and it had my picture in it. My mom reported me as a runaway. If they find me, they'll take me straight back—and I'll really be in trouble then."

"No!" Cara's breath caught at the thought of losing Zoe again. She squeezed her friend, pressing Zoe's bony frame tightly against her shoulder. She could feel her friend's chest rising and falling against her own. "Wait, what about my parents? If they find out, they'll call your parents in, like, one second. They are lawyers, after all."

Zoe nodded. "I know, I thought of that too. What if I just stay in your room? I won't go out, I'll be totally quiet. No one will ever know I'm here. You can just bring me up food sometimes . . ."

"We can hang out, talk . . ." Excitement was beginning to flood through Cara. "They work all the time anyway." She jumped up from the bed. "Zo, you have no idea what amazing timing this is. I really needed someone right now."

"I know you did. I could just feel it." Zoe stood up too and pulled Cara into a hug. For a long moment, they just stood together in the middle of the floor, their arms wrapped around each other. Cara could feel Zoe's heart beating in rhythm with her own. Zoe pulled away, her face lit up by a huge grin. "Okay, so tell me everything that's happened to you in the last seven years. Every detail!"

Cara dropped her arms and swiped at her eyes. "Not here. I have a better place." She led Zoe over to the window and raised the sash and then the screen. She climbed out onto the roof that spread just below the window, overlooking the side yard. Zoe followed. They settled on the rough asphalt shingles, still warm from the heat of the day. They sat with their backs resting comfortably against the clapboard, their arms looped around their updrawn knees. The autumn night was warm, and scented with the faint smell of wood smoke. Zoe sighed and tilted her head back against the wall, gazing up at the stars.

"I'm so glad I'm here. You have no idea what it was like, Cara, sneaking out of there, walking to the highway. I was so scared, people kept honking at me. I even lost my backpack."

"You don't have to worry anymore. You're safe here." Cara patted Zoe's knee.

Zoe raised her head and looked around, taking in the sprawling, manicured lawns and gracious homes all around them, perfectly illuminated by outdoor spotlights. Dark pockets of woods tastefully separated neighbors. At this hour, the only sounds were the soft *shush-shush* of automatic sprinklers. "I knew you'd have some kind of plush setup," Zoe noted. "You always did."

Before Cara could reply, a door slammed, and the quiet of the night was broken by the sound of girls' voices next door. "So, he was like, 'Oh my God, they're home,' and I wasn't wearing anything—," someone was saying loudly. A chorus of titters broke out. Girls clutching bottles of beer filtered out through glass doors onto the teak deck and collapsed onto the white linen lounge chairs surrounding the jewel-like swimming pool. Its sapphire water sparkled, illuminated by the yellow lights at the bottom.

Zoe raised an eyebrow at Cara. "My neighbor." Cara sighed. "Sydney. And her friends—"

Her words were cut off by the clatter of something metallic hitting the deck, followed by screams of laughter. Sydney, clad in a tight pink tank that clearly showed the outlines of her black bra, had knocked into one of the tables. She was currently trying to extricate herself from the grasp of a closed umbrella.

"That's Alexis, Sydney's best friend." Cara pointed to Alexis, who was laid out like an Egyptian princess on a lounge chair, posing as if she expected a paparazzo to appear out of nowhere and snap her picture. "She's the worst one. My parents are really close with hers, and they used to try and make us hang out when we first moved here. As soon as the grown-ups left the room, Alexis would call me Monkey-Face. She'd tell me I was too ugly for her to play with." Cara sighed. "Mom realized it was a lost cause after a while."

Down below, a short blonde named Maren appeared in the doorway of the kitchen, waving a pitcher of something pink over her head.

"Vodka slushes, everyone!" she called. There was a mad stampede to the pitcher. Maren filled big red plastic cups and handed them around. Someone burped and everyone giggled.

"You're so nasty, Erin!" Alexis called out. "Why don't you just show us your crack instead?"

Zoe looked over at Cara. "Is everyone at your school like this?"

Cara nodded. Then she paused. "Well, not everyone." She stared down at Sydney, but she could feel Zoe watching her. Finally, she looked over. Zoe had a mischievous little smile on her face.

"Okay, who is he?" Zoe teased. "Come on, spill."

Cara giggled. "Um, his name is Ethan. Tall, dark, handsome, incredibly sweet. Oh yeah—saved my life yesterday."

"What?" Zoe exclaimed.

"It was kind of amazing." She filled her friend in on the infamous choking incident, starting with Ethan's strong arms around her waist—and ending with her new nickname. "And now they call me *Choker*," she finished. "Talk about literally adding insult to injury. Basically, Alexis and Sydney think I'm the biggest freak in school." Cara felt a hot wave of shame build in her chest, even here, alone with Zoe. "It's been like this since I got here. Middle school was awful, but I hoped to start fresh in high school. Yeah, right. In ninth grade, there was this freshman fall dance. I was so excited, my first real high school event." Cara paused. She thought of the red velvet dress with the gold sequin bodice she'd worn, not realizing everyone else would be in jeans and tight little tops. It was the reason she now wore a uniform of khakis and T-shirts. "And whatever, I was clueless, right? I was just a little freshman."

Zoe nodded. Her eyes shone in the dark like a cat's.

"So I asked this guy, Marc Simons, to dance. I thought he was really cute—he was wearing a leather jacket."

"Ohhh, the height of coolness!" Zoe laughed.

"I know, I thought it was great. So I ask this guy to dance, and he said 'no.' Just like that, right in front of everyone." Cara's fingers tightened on the gritty asphalt shingles.

"What a jerk!" Zoe shook her head.

"Anyway, Alexis and Sydney saw the whole thing, and they basically followed me around for the next six months, calling me Mrs. Simons, asking if Marc had called." She shrugged. "It never stops. Posting crap about me on Facebook, prank calls. Honestly, I'm kind of used to it by now. I'm even used to Alexis and Ethan being together." But even as the words came out of her mouth, she knew it wasn't true. Zoe squeezed Cara's knee.

36

"Bitches," she said, waving her hand in dismissal. "Fake bitches."

Cara grinned and rearranged her legs on the rough shingles. Beneath them, the party was getting loud. There was the crash of breaking glass, and a splash. "Maren is in the pool!" someone yelled.

"God, that sucks about Alexis and Ethan." Zoe sucked in her cheeks, thinking. "If only they'd break up. Maybe we can find a way to help them along. . . ."

Cara snorted. "Right. We can start working on my presidential campaign right after that."

Just then, someone yelled "Choker!" from the deck next door. Cara panicked. She looked down, expecting the girls to have spotted them. Instead, they were still sitting in their lounge chairs, watching as Sydney staggered around, grabbing her throat with both hands and bugging out her eyes.

"She sounded like this!" she yelled before letting out a series of retches and gags, like a calf with its throat slit. Everyone broke out into hysterical laughter. Alexis snorted some of her vodka slush up her nose and had to be pounded on the back until she recovered.

Cara and Zoe watched in silence. Sydney staggered for another minute before dropping into a lounge chair herself. "Hey, remember when she started crying in the hall because she couldn't get her locker open?" she said, her voice carrying up as if she was sitting right there on the roof with them. The other girls tittered in response. Cara looked straight ahead at the trees across the street. She remembered perfectly. That was also freshman year.

Below her, Maren's languid drawl chimed in. "How about

when she got that bloody nose in volleyball and her mom had to come get her. . . ."

Cara's palms were sweating. She didn't dare look at Zoe.

Then she felt a soft hand on her shoulder. "Things must have been really hard for you," Zoe said softly.

"It's been awful," Cara admitted, letting out a sigh. "When we were growing up, and my parents were never around, at least I had you there. And then, after we moved, they spent all this time with me, which was great. But of course it didn't last. It's like they got tired of me or something. Now they're always working, just like before. Honestly . . . I'm all alone." It was amazing how good it felt to tell someone the truth—as if she'd been holding her breath for a long time and could finally, finally exhale.

"You *were* all alone," Zoe corrected her. She squeezed Cara's hand.

Beneath them, a cell rang and Sydney grabbed her phone. "Oh my God, it's Jack!" she squealed.

"Why's he calling *you*?" Alexis sniped.

"Shut up." Sydney already had the phone to her ear. "Hello? Do you guys mind? Can I have a little privacy here?"

The other girls slowly peeled themselves off the lounge chairs, trailing back into the house. Alexis was the last one in. "Don't stay out too late, slut!" she called over her shoulder. Sydney gave her the finger without looking around. Alexis giggled and slid the doors shut, leaving Sydney alone by the pool.

Cara felt Zoe's warm hand creep over hers. "You don't have to worry about anything now, Car." Zoe squeezed her palm. "I'm here now. I'll take care of you."

Chapter 5

$\mathcal{T}$HE GIRLS CLAMBERED BACK THROUGH THE WINDOW. Cara brushed her hand over the pebbly imprint the asphalt shingles had left on the back of her legs. Her room was warm and welcoming after the chilly darkness of the roof. Zoe stretched her arms high above her head. "I'm exhausted." She yawned, sinking down on the edge of the bed. She flopped over backward, almost hidden by the puffy, black-and-white striped pillows and comforter billowing up around her.

Cara bustled around, getting a clean towel out of the bathroom, rummaging around for pajamas for Zoe. "So, I think you're going to be fine here. I mean, this room is so big, it's like your own hotel suite—"

"Car." Zoe cut her off. "Please shut up."

Cara looked over at her friend, wounded. Zoe was still buried in the bedclothes, staring up at the ceiling.

"I've been through a lot today. Can we save the celebrating until tomorrow?"

Cara handed her a gray T-shirt and a pair of old gym

shorts. "Of course." She leaned over and hugged her friend. "I'm just so, so glad you're here. It's amazing you showed up just when I really needed someone. But then again, you always knew when something was wrong. Remember when I was so mad Mom wouldn't let me go to the May Fest at school?"

"In fifth grade." Zoe spoke without moving.

"And I went over to your house and we made our own roller coaster?"

"Out of that washing machine box and all that old wire." Zoe smiled from her sprawled-out position.

Cara pulled on a tank top and a pair of boxers and climbed under the covers. "Hey, move over—you're hogging the bed. I'm having flashbacks to our sleepovers." She nudged Zoe's knee with her own.

"Mmmm," Zoe mumbled. She shifted a few inches to the right.

Cara eased down a little farther between the sheets. She lay for a moment, staring into the darkness, listening to Zoe's breathing beside her.

Just this morning, she'd risen from this same bed, her throat aching from the choking incident, feeling like she was going to vomit all over again at the prospect of facing everyone at school. But with Zoe here, that fear seemed silly. Cara yawned luxuriously and hitched the comforter up around her neck. She closed her eyes and felt herself slide almost immediately into sleep. Then a voice jolted her back.

"Cara?"

She opened her eyes. "What?"

Zoe raised her head, her black hair tangled across her face. "Will you pet my hair? Remember? Like you used to?"

"I remember." All those nights when Zoe would climb in her window, crying because of her stepdad. She would get into bed, and Cara would stroke her hair, over and over, the shiny black strands slick under her fingers, until Zoe's crying finally ceased and her breathing deepened.

Cara turned on her side and softly placed her hand on Zoe's head. Her hair felt just like it used to in fourth grade, silky and smooth. She petted her head over and over.

"That's so nice," Zoe mumbled, her face to the wall. She was already half asleep. Cara smiled to herself and listened to Zoe's breathing for a long time before she finally fell asleep herself.

She dreamed there was a fire at school. The alarm bells were beeping in deafening blasts. The hallway was full of smoke and running, screaming kids. And she was standing in the middle of it all, choking again on the carrot. But this time, no one noticed. They were all too busy running from the fire. Cara saw Ethan run past her dream-self, and she opened her mouth and tried to scream for him, but nothing came out. She knew it this time, her mind blared. This time she was going to die. The fire alarm grew louder and louder.

Cara opened her eyes. The room was bathed in red light, and for a brief instant, she thought her dream had been real. Then the blaring noise grew louder, as if it were coming from inside the room. Cara sat up and glanced over at Zoe. She was still in the same position, apparently undisturbed by the noise, buried in the pillow.

Cara threw back the comforter and shivered her way to the window. The floorboards felt slick and icy under her feet. The blaring abruptly stopped. Cara peered through the glass. An ambulance was pulled up in front of Sydney's house, its siren silenced but the lights still flashing. Two EMTs leaped from the front seat and ran up the steps. One carried a big black case, while the other had an orange tote bag slung over his shoulder. The bigger EMT rang the doorbell. When there was no answer, they both peered through the sidelights, then tried the door, which opened. Cara watched them disappear inside.

She turned back to the bed. "Zoe!" She shook her friend's shoulder.

"Hmm, wha?" Zoe mumbled without opening her eyes. She rolled over and tried to pull the pillow over her head.

Cara shook her again and pulled the comforter off. "Get up! Something's happening next door."

Zoe sat up. "Oh my God, what? I'm sleeping!" She moaned, rubbing at her face.

"Jesus, you're hard to wake up. Something's wrong at Sydney's. There's an ambulance outside." Cara returned to the window as Zoe swung her legs to the floor. "The paramedics went inside."

"Car, look here."

Cara turned away from the window. Zoe was standing at the other window, the one that looked out over Sydney's deck. Cara went over to her and peered out. Illuminated like a sculpture in the sapphire water, a body floated facedown in the pool. The pool lights sent up gorgeous beams of gold, like columns supporting the prone form.

The figure's long brown hair spread out across the water like seaweed. She wore a pink tank top with a black bra underneath and white skinny jeans. Cara's fingers curled against the windowsill. A faint whiff of chlorine wafted by her nose. "Oh my God, it's Sydney," she whispered.

Zoe stood silently beside her. As they watched, the EMTs burst through the back doors of the house, followed by a screaming Alexis.

"She's there! She's there!" they heard Alexis shriek, pointing at the pool. Her hair stood out from her head as if she'd been electrocuted. The EMTs used the pool cleaning pole to propel Sydney's body to the side and hauled her from the water with a hand under each armpit. Cara felt bile rise in her throat as Sydney's limp form was dragged over the edge, streaming water across the pool deck. Her head flopped limply onto her shoulder.

"Oh my God! Oh my God!" Alexis screamed over and over. The EMTs laid Sydney out on the deck. One pumped her chest with his bare hands, while the other began pulling things out of the orange tote bag. Behind them, the other partygoers stood in a cluster just inside the glass doors, holding one another tight.

Then Cara's mother emerged from a gap in the hedge that divided the two houses, Cara's father close behind. Mom had a pashmina draped over one arm, and Dad was still wearing his suit. They must have just come home from their event. Mom clicked over to the EMTs, balancing on her stilettos. Her hand went to her mouth, and she uttered a stifled little shriek as she caught sight of Sydney's body. One of the EMTs looked up. "Are you the parents of this girl?" His hands were still pressed on Sydney's chest.

"No," Mom said, her eyes fixed on the body. "Oh dear. We're the neighbors. We were just coming home and heard the disturbance. . . ." Her voice trailed off as she stared at Sydney's body. Dad put an arm around her shoulders.

"Will she be okay, sir?" he asked the EMT. The man didn't answer.

"It's too soon to tell," the other EMT responded. "We'd appreciate it if you could go back home. Thanks." He pulled out a long tube and began doing something near Sydney's head.

Mom and Dad made their way back through the hedge. A moment later, Cara heard her own front door open and close, and then their footsteps as they moved around downstairs. Her own breath was coming fast and shallow. She realized she was holding Zoe's hand. Her friend's grip was strong and reassuring.

Footsteps were coming up the stairs. Cara's heart beat short and fast as she realized her parents were going to check on her. Her eyes met Zoe's, and as if reading her mind, her friend dropped like a stone to the carpet and rolled under the bed in one swift movement.

Cara threw herself onto the bed and pulled the covers up around her neck just as a soft knock came at the door. She closed her eyes and forced herself to inhale deeply and slowly. She flung one arm over her head in an attitude of sleep. Beneath the bed, Zoe was completely silent.

Eyes closed, Cara heard the door open a crack. She knew her mom must be peeking in, but didn't dare look. There was a pause of about ten years, and then the door gently shut. Cara didn't open her eyes until she heard footsteps receding back down the stairs.

Zoe slid out from under the dust ruffle, a dustball clinging to her hair. "I guess I'm initiated now."

"Seriously." Cara exhaled and made her way back to the window. "That was a close one."

Outside, the EMTs were still working on Sydney. They'd turned her head to one side. She still wasn't moving. Over and over, they pressed on her chest, then squeezed a blue bag they had attached to a tube in her mouth. Finally, one EMT got up, leaving the other one to continue CPR, and drew Alexis to the side. His words floated up on the cool autumn air. "So just how much did your friend have to drink?" he asked.

"I don't know," Alexis said woodenly. She stood in front of him, twisting her hands, her huge eyes locked on Sydney's still form. "I don't know, we were all drinking. She had a lot, I guess. I fell asleep. Is she dead? Oh my God, is she dead?" Her voice rose to a hysterical scream. She pushed at the EMT suddenly, trying to shove him aside to get over to Sydney. He caught her by the shoulders.

"All right, I know you're upset. Where are her parents?" He poised a pen over a small notebook.

"They're gone. They're at their country place," Alexis sobbed. "Please tell me, please tell me, is she dead?"

"Oh my God, freak-out alert," Zoe muttered. "Somebody give the girl some Xanax." Cara giggled involuntarily, then clapped a hand over her mouth, horrified at herself.

The EMT snapped his notebook closed. He nodded at the other EMT, who rose from his crouched position next to Sydney's form and raised a radio to his mouth. He said something unintelligible into the speaker. They lifted Sydney onto a hard orange stretcher and secured her body with straps. Cara's breath caught as they pulled a sheet up over her face.

So that was it. She was dead.

Alexis had fallen silent. She stared at Sydney's body on the stretcher, still covered by the sheet. With the silent efficiency of furniture movers, the EMTs hoisted the stretcher and maneuvered it around the tumbled deck furniture and through the side gate to the front of the house.

Cara sank down on her bed as the sirens started up again and then wailed away into the night. She took a deep, shaky breath. "Oh my God. I can't believe this," she said. The scene outside had an air of unreality. As if the whole thing had been part of her dream.

Zoe sat down next to her. "I know. She must have tripped and fallen in, right?"

Cara nodded. "I guess so. She was really drunk." She shivered violently at the memory of Sydney's head swinging limply when they dragged her out of the pool.

Cara closed her eyes and felt Zoe's warm hand on her hair, stroking it over and over. At last, she was able to lie down again on the bed, and a long time after that, she fell into a deep, dreamless sleep.

Chapter 6

THE ANNOUNCEMENT CAME OVER THE PA DURING homeroom on Monday morning. *"All students are to report to the gym immediately for a mandatory assembly,"* the tinny voice of Ms. Sitwell declared. Cara's eyes darted around the room. She'd been waiting for news of Sydney's death since walking into the lobby half an hour ago. But no one seemed concerned. Students rose from their seats, talking, cramming notebooks into their bags. Alexis's seat was glaringly empty.

"Tell me what they say at school," Zoe had urged as Cara left that morning.

"Are you sure you're going to be okay?" Cara asked for the hundredth time.

Zoe had sat cross-legged on the bed, the covers rumpled up around her waist. Her face was puffy in the seven o'clock light. "Stop being such a mommy. Look, I have snacks, magazines, the laptop. I'm set—now go, or you're going to be late." Zoe waved her toward the door.

Now Cara hoisted her backpack onto her shoulders as

she made her way through the sea of people toward the gym. The red-drenched scene in her memory seemed more dream-like than ever in the light of day, eclipsed by mundane concerns like finding clean underwear and drinking orange juice at breakfast. But Zoe had been there—she saw it all too. It really had happened.

The enormous steel gym bleachers were packed when Cara arrived. She squeezed onto a corner of a bench next to two freshman girls, each listening to one earphone of an iPod. There was a deafening roar as everyone shouted to one another, rummaged through backpacks, and texted their friends, even though cells were forbidden during school hours. Cara quickly scanned the crowd for Alexis. She didn't see her. Her eyes landed on the rest of the girls from the party sitting close together on a top bleacher, whispering to one another. No one else seemed to notice anything was amiss.

"People, people!" Mr. Barre, the principal, stood in front of them, his bald head shining as though it had been waxed. He was flanked by two women and a man in slacks and a sweater, as well as the guidance counselor, Mrs. Laudeman. He tapped the microphone in front of him. "Hello? Is this on? Hello?"

The physics teacher jogged up and turned the switch at the base of the microphone. He offered Mr. Barre a smile before jogging back.

"Thanks, Rob." The mike whined and some students covered their ears. Mr. Barre cleared his throat. One by one, everyone fell silent. "Students, I'm afraid I have some sad news for you this morning. One of our juniors, Sydney Powers, died at her home this past Friday night."

A collective gasp passed through the crowd. One of the little

48

freshmen next to Cara pressed both hands to her mouth. Mr. Barre opened his mouth to continue but was interrupted by the bang of one of the gym doors. Everyone's heads swiveled as one.

Cara straightened up at the sight of Alexis staggering in, Ethan at her side. He had his arm around her, steadying her, since she seemed barely able to walk. The students were quiet, as if waiting for a performance to start. "I can't believe she's gone. I can't believe she's gone," Alexis muttered over and over in a trembling voice.

Ethan guided Alexis to a space in the front row. People gave them respectful glances as they moved aside to make room. *Like she was her freaking sister or something,* Cara thought. She caught herself. Alexis's best friend was dead, after all. She chided herself for being so cruel. That was more like something Zoe would say.

At the front, Mr. Barre cleared his throat and went on. "We're going to miss Sydney, who was a cheerleader and a tireless supporter of this school."

Tireless supporter of her bitchy friends, Cara imagined Zoe saying. She could almost see her friend next to her on the bleachers, sneaking gummy worms out of her backpack and doodling on her sneakers the way she used to in fifth grade. Cara shook her head violently, drawing a curious glance from the little freshmen.

Mr. Barre went on. "We know this loss will be difficult, so we have arranged for counselors from the Lifespring Center for Grief to meet with students who so desire immediately following this assembly. And of course, our own guidance counselor, Mrs. Laudeman, will also be available to anyone who would like to talk." He gestured to the people standing behind him, who stepped forward. There was a general rustling and murmuring as students stood up and started gathering their things. A handful trickled down to the counselors in the front. Mrs. Laudeman arranged them in small groups.

Cara stood up and grabbed her backpack. The odor of ancient sweat and gym shoes hung in the air. She could feel a trickle of sweat start at her neck and run down into her bra. She stumbled down the concrete steps, once painted white, now worn to a smooth brown gloss from thirty years of sneakers. People stood in the way, choking the aisle. Stupid people, all talking, blocking the way. *The smell*. It was getting stronger.

"Excuse me," Cara said to a girl in a one-shoulder blouse in front of her. The girl didn't hear her. Forget it. Cara pushed past her, but her toe caught on a corner of the bottom bleacher. She stumbled. A pair of hands caught her by the upper arms.

"Careful there!" Mrs. Laudeman said in her strong, take-charge voice.

Cara resisted the urge to pull her arms away. Mrs. Laudeman smiled and released her grip. "Do you want to join one of the small groups, Cara?"

The muscle at the corner of her eye jumped. Cara shook her head. "I have a class," she mumbled, brushing past the counselor. Her eye was twitching like mad now.

As she struggled through the mass toward the door, she passed Alexis sitting on a blue plastic chair, Ethan standing next to her. One of the counselors knelt in front of her, holding her hands. Some of the other girls from the party were clustered close behind.

"I don't know how I'm going to go on living without her,"

Alexis was sobbing. Her eyes were so swollen from crying they looked like little slits. Ethan patted her shoulder, his face downcast.

"Sydney seemed like she was much loved by her friends," the counselor said in a professional, soothing voice.

"Oh, she was!" Maren piped up. "She was so much fun. And so sweet."

"Yeah, she'd do anything for you," Erin chimed in. There were collective nods.

"The best thing any of you can do for Sydney is to carry her legacy with you." The counselor was addressing the group now, looking pointedly at each face as she spoke. Everyone nodded vigorously.

Cara exhaled through her nose and continued her fight toward the door. God, if she could just get outside. She had her hand on the push bar of the doors when the microphone behind her started up again.

The feedback whined. Cara turned around reluctantly. A burly football player Cara vaguely recognized was standing at the mike, his hands stuffed awkwardly in his jeans pockets. His name was Mike or Mack or something. He leaned over.

"Hey, everyone." His voice boomed through the gym. The chatter dropped to a hum. People turned around. "So, Homecoming starts on Thursday. And you know, Sydney was a cheerleader and a huge fan of our school, so—" He cleared his throat. "So, you know—"

Get to the point, Mike. Mack.

"—I just want to encourage everyone who has games and meets this weekend to play for Sydney." His voice rose at the end of the sentence, bouncing off the walls, and he raised his arm in a fisted salute while everyone else broke into cheers.

In one swift motion, Cara turned around and slammed through the heavy doors, the fresh air blowing against her face at last. Breathing heavily, her fists clenched, she took a fast lap around the parking lot, her sneakers slapping the smooth black asphalt. At last, she slowed. She could feel her eye gradually stop twitching. Cara leaned her head on a nearby Explorer, the sun-warmed roof hot under her forehead. Tears suddenly pricked her eyes. Sydney was dead and everyone was acting like she was the most beloved person in school.

Stop worrying about those jerks, Cara, she imagined Zoe saying. *They're not worth your time.*

What if she herself died? Cara thought. No one would even notice. Her parents would, but they'd probably be relieved they wouldn't have to talk to their awkward teenage daughter anymore. Cara lifted her head and drew her knuckle across her eyes.

Well, at least one person would care. Zoe would miss her.

Chapter 7

O N Thursday night, Cara crouched at the side of the track in the warm-up area, stretching her right hamstring. She pressed her forehead to her knee, trying to ignore the bubbling feeling in her stomach.

Above her, moths swarmed the big halogen lights, committing ritual suicide by flying directly into the hot bulbs. The shiny metal bleachers seemed to float in the black night like a silvery ship, friends and parents bundled in colorful parkas scattered throughout. It was a pretty big crowd for track, probably because it was Homecoming. Her parents, naturally, were working. A big deposition, Mom said. Absolutely essential that she be there. It was okay by Cara. They didn't need to be here for this train wreck.

Carefully, Cara tucked her right leg under her and stretched out her left. It felt a little tighter than the right. She flexed her foot and reached for the toe of her spikes. Bending over made her stomach feel worse. Out in the grassy center, the long jumpers were sprinting up their jump path over and over. The sand pit in front of them was still smooth and unmarked. Cara could hear the grunt of Sammy Nelson, the shot putter, as he flung the heavy iron ball with a thud into the grass.

Runners were standing and sitting in their blue and white warm-ups. No sign of Ethan, though. He must still be in the locker room. Coach Sanders walked by, rapidly flipping pages on his clipboard. Cara watched as his blue-nyloned legs stopped near her. "Lange, the four hundred is first up." His disembodied voice came from up high.

Cara made her head nod and watched as his legs tramped away. She bent her head toward her leg, feeling the muscle in her calf cramp slightly. *Oh God, don't let me choke. Not at Homecoming.* Her last couple of races had been . . . not so good. A greasy sheen of sweat broke out on her forehead as she thought of the meet against Racine. Her feet glued to the starting blocks. The sharp crack of the gun. The backs of her teammates receding down the track. She'd hobbled over to the sidelines, claiming a massive leg cramp, and even though no one said anything, Cara could feel them looking at her in the locker room after the meet, and whispering.

Not tonight, not tonight. Things were different now. Zoe was here. Cara closed her eyes and tried to summon the strength of her friend at home. Zoe wouldn't be scared. She'd burn up the track. Cara felt the cramp in her calf loosen and, with a wave of relief, pressed her head all the way down to her knee. Her hamstring didn't feel tight anymore.

Cara stood up and leaned against the chain-link fence. She dug a piece of peppermint gum out of her pocket and popped it into her mouth. The sharp bite of the mint cooled her tongue. Slowly, the sick feeling in her stomach dissipated.

A breeze blew by her face, with a hint of wood smoke from distant bonfires.

Nearby laughter rose in a puff on the wind. Sarit, Rachael, and Julie were clustered a few yards away, their heads together. Sarit gestured at her throat as she murmured to the others. Cara's heart sank. Not here. Not after this awful week, and right before her race. She tried to arrange her face into an "I don't care" expression, but she knew it looked like a mask. Whatever strength she'd channeled from Zoe flowed away.

Then Rachael stepped to one side to fix her shoe, and the group's words floated over to Cara more clearly. "Apparently, she refuses to take it off," she heard Madeline say. The other girls shook their heads, their hands pressed to their mouths.

"Does Alexis think wearing Sydney's necklace is going to bring her back or something?" Julie's eyes were wide.

Cara sagged against the fence. No one was talking about her. *Get a grip, Cara,* she thought of Zoe saying. *It's not always about you.* Just then, she caught sight of Ethan weaving his way across the field. The light shone on his dark hair. His blue warm-ups, the same color as everyone else's, seemed to glow. Cara's breath came more quickly as he drew near.

"Hey, Cara," he said as he passed her.

Cara opened her mouth but closed it without saying anything. Like saying something was even an option when she was so entirely lost in his scent of Right Guard deodorant and warm skin.

A blast from Coach Sanders's whistle scattered the spell. "All right, runners, over here!" The team clustered around the coach like a swarm of shiny blue nylon fish.

"Franklin is fast and tough," Coach Sanders said. "You

all are going to have to put forth your very best." He waved his clipboard at the opposite end of the field, where Franklin, clad in red, was warming up. Cara took a look at them for the first time. They did look tough—and *tall*. One girl in particular had legs like stilts. She was bent down, touching her toes with her ankles crossed. She looked like a grazing giraffe.

"Competitors to watch." Coach Sanders consulted his clipboard. "Kohli, hundred meters—keep your eye on number eighteen. She was first in regionals last year."

Sarit nodded confidently, her long dark ponytail bobbing. "No problem."

"Lange, watch number six. She's extremely fast at the start." He waved his clipboard, and Cara followed his arm in the direction of the giraffe girl. Oh God. Not her. Not in the Homecoming meet. Cara gulped. Coach Sanders apparently took that as a "yes," because he went on. "Okay, folks, that's it. It's almost time. Four hundred meter runners, go to the starting line." He waved his clipboard at them, and the runners scattered, trailing back toward the track.

Cara's feet carried her toward the start line. She could barely feel them touching the ground. The chatter of the other runners and the occasional cheers from the crowd receded, leaving only the roar of blood in her ears.

The other runners were already at the start, one per lane—three from her own team and four from Franklin. Number six was at the end. Cara crouched and pressed her feet firmly against the rubber of the blocks. She could feel the grit of the track under her fingertips. The starter raised his gun in the air. For one awful moment, Cara felt her stomach rise. *Oh God, no, not now.* Her legs had that terrible heavy feeling.

Then Zoe's face flashed into her head. The starter gun went off. *Go!* Zoe mouthed in Cara's mind.

Cara felt her legs lurch away from the blocks. Before she could think, she was hurtling down the track. She could feel her legs pistoning in time with the rapid thump of her pulse. Rounding the first turn. She leaned to the inside, fighting to stay upright. Two runners pounded beside her. Cara couldn't see them except for a flash of red and one of blue. Six, where was six? She couldn't see her.

The straightaway. Faintly, she registered the yelling of the crowd. Approaching the second turn. Cara's legs slowed slightly, and with all of her strength, Cara forced them back to their original pace. There was only one runner ahead of her. Where were the others? Did they already finish? The final stretch. Breath whistled through her open mouth, and with a final push, she forced her legs over the white finish line looming in front of her. "All right, Cara!" she faintly heard someone yell, and then a cheer.

Her legs pounded the pavement more and more slowly. In a flash, Cara realized there was only one person ahead of her at the finish line, a willowy blonde in red—number ten. The red giraffe was *behind* her. And all the other runners were too, including the three from her own team. Which meant . . . she'd actually come in second, and first on her own team. Cara felt a bubble of joy rise in her chest, lifting her up like a giant helium balloon.

She came to a halt, resting with her hands on her knees. Her lungs fought the sudden stop, trying to expand in her chest. Cara pulled herself upright, putting her hands behind her head to give her lungs as much room to breathe as possible.

She walked in a small circle before looking around. Someone clapped her on the back. Cara stumbled and almost fell over.

"Nice work, Cara!" Julie cried.

"Yeah, good job," Sarit chimed in. She raised her hand, and tentatively Cara slapped her palm. A few other people reached out to pat her back as she passed. Cara nodded at them, trying to keep what she hoped was a nonchalant expression on her face—as if almost winning during Homecoming was no big deal. In fact, she was wearing a big sloppy grin, but she couldn't help it. And for once, she didn't care.

The deserted warm-up area was a sea of discarded blue nylon and open gym bags. Ethan was perched on a cooler, scribbling madly in a calculus notebook. He looked up as Cara approached. "Nice race," he said and held up his hand. Cara's heart gave a giant thud. She willed her eye not to start twitching.

"Thanks, Ethan," she said as casually as she could and awkwardly tried to slap his palm. But oh God, her hand missed his, actually *missed* it, and she wound up slapping the air next to his hand. She almost lost her balance, but caught herself before she actually stumbled into his knees. She could feel her face turning into a red map of splotches. She resisted the urge to flee and let out an idiotic little giggle instead. "Um, can I try that again?"

Ethan's eyes crinkled at the edges. He held up his hand and Cara slapped it. "Better," he said, smiling.

Yes, much better.

Chapter 8

THE COOL NIGHT AIR ENVELOPED CARA AS SHE FLOATED home after the meet. A police car wailed past, its red lights flashing, but she barely noticed. Not when Ethan's sweet smile was dancing in front of her.

The windows were dark at home, but her parents' cars were in the garage.

Inside, there was a line of light under Mom's office door. Cara poked her head in. Her mother was staring intently at a page of densely packed legal text, a glass of Scotch beside her. Samson was curled up on a stack of law journals on the floor. From the Bose sound dock in the corner, Bob Dylan was wailing softly.

"Knock, knock," Cara said from the doorway.

Her mother swung around. She wore a hooded gray IU sweatshirt and sweatpants, black reading glasses perched at the edge of her nose. There was a smear of red pen on her chin. "Oh hi, honey," she said. "How was the meet?"

"Good, actually." Cara grinned. "I came in second." She

took a step into the room and perched on the worn arm of a green velour armchair.

"Uh-hmm. Listen, honey, I wanted to talk to you about something." Mom's voice dropped. She took off her glasses.

"What?" Cara crossed her arms over her chest.

Mom tapped a pen on the desk. "It's nothing really. Earlier in the week when I was passing your room, I just heard you . . . talking to yourself." She cleared her throat.

Heat rushed to Cara's face. She'd heard her talking to Zoe. She walked over to the bookcase and studied the titles. "Mom, was it at night?" Her voice sounded calm. "Because you know I talk in my sleep." *Evidence, Second Edition,* she read.

"Yes . . . I remember that." Cara heard a creak as Mom shifted her weight in the chair. "I was wondering if the, er, passing of Sydney had . . . upset you." She seemed to be choosing her words with unusual care.

Cara let out a breath. Her mom didn't suspect Zoe. "Yeah. Um, it's been kind of weird at school. I think a lot of people are upset." She patted her mother on the shoulder. "But I'm cool. Thanks for asking."

"Oh, good." Mom sounded relieved. She picked up her sheaf of legal papers. "I overheard Chief Rangleif down at the courthouse today. Apparently, they're still investigating Sydney's death."

Cara frowned. "What's there to investigate? She was drunk and fell in the pool."

Her mother shook her head. "I didn't catch everything he was saying, but apparently the investigation isn't closed.

60

That's all I know." Her eyes drifted back to the papers. She picked up a highlighter and ran it across a line. "Leftover Chinese in the fridge."

Cara stood a moment longer, gazing at the back of her mother's bent head, then turned and slowly trailed out of the room.

After extracting the carton of shrimp lo mein, Cara climbed the stairs, sticking a fork into the slippery noodles. Samson, who had a lifelong obsession with soy sauce, followed. Cara breathed a sigh of relief when she saw her bedroom door firmly shut. She didn't know what she was worried about—maybe that Zoe would've left. Cara didn't think she could stand that. It had only been a week, but already she was back to depending on Zoe. Before she did anything, she needed to know what she thought. Just like when they were little. When she'd open presents at her birthday parties, her first thought was always if Zoe would like the toy or book inside. If Zoe didn't approve of something, Cara would throw it away.

Cara twisted the knob and pushed open the door. Zoe was sitting on the floor, her back against Cara's bed, a magazine propped on her knees. She looked up with a huge smile. "Hey, you're home!" She jumped up and gave Cara a big sloppy kiss on the cheek.

Cara grinned. Samson nudged her foot, trying to slip past her into the room. "No," she told him and shoved him back.

"Wait, who's this?" Zoe looked down. "Aw, you didn't tell me you had a cat. Hi, cutie." Samson twitched his tail back and forth, and Zoe scooped him up, cradling him like a baby. The cat's belly hung to one side. He grunted.

Cara grimaced. "He's my mother's. And he's not cute, he's

fat and smelly and he sheds on everything. My mother loves him though. More than me, I think."

"Well, duh!" Zoe laughed at the stricken look on Cara's face and tenderly set Samson on his feet in the hall. "Night-night, bunny," she crooned.

She plopped down on the striped comforter and tugged Cara down next to her. "So, what happened today? I've been so bored. You have to tell me everything. How was the meet?"

Cara sank back on the pillows and tucked a hand behind her head. "Well, first of all, guess what Mom just told me?"

"What?"

"The police are still investigating Sydney's death." She widened her eyes at Zoe dramatically.

Zoe's brow wrinkled in confusion. "What are they investigating? Drunk people drown all the time."

"I know." Cara shrugged. "Maybe she hit her head or something. I don't know. Her parents could sue the pool manufacturers."

"Okay, so tell me about today!" Zoe changed the subject. "You looked really happy when you came in, so good things must have happened."

"Oh, they did. The meet was awesome." Cara recounted her unexpected second-place finish and the congratulations from her teammates, concluding with her botched hand-slap with Ethan. "So, what do you think? Do you think he thinks I'm an idiot who can't even high-five someone?"

Zoe pursed her mouth, thinking. "You said he smiled after you missed his hand?"

"Yeah. What? Is that good? Or bad? Is it bad?" She waited anxiously.

Zoe tapped her fingertip on her cheek. "Nooo, I don't think it's bad. Actually, he might be thinking you're cute, in a kind of innocent way." She studied Cara a moment. "You know, maybe you'd feel more confident with Ethan if you did something different with your hair. Have you ever thought about that?"

Cara touched her ponytail. "Well, sometimes. I mean, plain brown hair is kind of boring. But I don't know what to do with it."

Zoe sat up suddenly. "Here, let me see your hair." Zoe reached out for her, her long fingernails grazing Cara's neck. Instinctively Cara pulled away.

Zoe looked wounded. "You were always pulling away from me, you know that? Ever since we were little. Maybe that's why you abandoned me." She eyed Cara.

"What are you talking about? We moved!"

"Well, you left me, and my life was awful. You knew it too." Zoe laid her head back on the pillow and stared at the ceiling.

Cara felt her pulse speed up. "It wasn't easy for me either, you know. I was so upset about losing you, my parents made me talk to someone when we first moved here. I felt like *you'd* abandoned me."

"Oh yeah, and are you still seeing the guy now?"

"No . . . I felt better once I got adjusted to living here." Cara shifted. She felt almost guilty, though she knew she shouldn't. It had been her parents' decision to move, not hers. Besides, she'd written Zoe a few letters. She'd just sort of stopped after a while. But it wasn't like she'd forgotten about her friend completely. It was just that it was the "good period" then, and she was busy with her parents and building a new life. . . .

Instead of replying, Zoe reached over and pulled out Cara's hair band. Her lank brown locks fell around her shoulders. Her hair had gotten really long in the last year, and now it reached almost to the bottom of her shoulder blades.

Zoe tucked the ends under and leaned back, squinting at Cara. Standing so close, Cara could feel the heat coming off Zoe's body. "That's sort of it . . . ," Zoe said. She fluffed the top layer and held the bottom back behind Cara's neck.

"I'm in your hands," Cara said.

Zoe squealed. "Really? Can I do anything I want?"

Cara nodded. "Yeah. It can't get any worse, right?"

Zoe clapped her hands. "Makeover! Oh my God, this is going to be so fun." She bounded over to Cara's laptop on the desk. "Okay, first thing, and most important—makeover music." She scrolled through the iTunes list.

Cara climbed off the bed and opened the cabinet under the bathroom sink. "What supplies do you need?" she called.

"Scissors, a mirror, a flatiron, and the blow-dryer," Zoe called over her shoulder. "Madonna! Perfect." "Like a Virgin" filled the room. "Like a virgin, touched for the very first time," Madonna sang.

Oh, perfect for me, Cara thought as she extracted the flatiron from the back of the sink cabinet. "My parents are going to think I've turned into someone else," she said. "I hardly ever listen to that one."

"They won't come up here, will they?" Zoe sounded a little worried. She turned the music down a notch.

Cara tugged the flatiron hard from the cabinet, knocking

over several shampoo bottles in the process. "No, don't worry," she called back, spitting her hair from her face. "My mom actually heard us the other day—but she thinks I'm talking in my sleep. Anyway, she's more than happy buried in her office downstairs." She rose to her feet and blew some dust off the flatiron. "Here." She handed it to Zoe. "I haven't used it in, um, maybe ever. And look, I even found a mascara and some lip gloss. They're probably a hundred years old."

"Okay, then this is the start of your new life." Zoe arranged Cara in front of her dresser mirror and spread a towel over her shoulders. She poised a pair of scissors.

"Wait!" Cara clutched at her friend's hand. "You're going to cut it dry?"

"Of course. That's what all the top stylists do." Zoe sounded supremely confident. She easily broke her hand from Cara's grasp. "You'll look great with a buzz cut. I'll just get some clippers—"

"What!"

Zoe laughed. "Kidding! Now, shut up and relax. It's going to be amazing."

Cara closed her eyes as Zoe snipped a lock of hair at the back. She was going fast. The chunks of hair falling to the floor felt ominously heavy, but Cara refused to open her eyes. She heard Zoe put the scissors down and the cold mist of spray on her head. Then Zoe's firm fingers fluffing her hair, and the click as the flatiron warmed up. "Even though you have straight hair, the iron will get rid of all that frizz and make it shiny," Zoe said as she closed the hot plates on a section of hair.

"Ah! It's hot!" Cara gasped, squeezing her eyes, still tightly shut. She smelled the acrid stench of burning hair. "Oh God, don't burn my hair off, Zoe," she begged.

"Sorry, sorry! I'm turning it down," Zoe said. She methodically moved around Cara's head. After a few more minutes, she drew the iron away. "Okay, that's it. Open."

Cara opened her eyes. There in the mirror was a girl with a plain, pale face like her own, but now capped with a rough, messy bob. It was kind of rocker-girl cool. She turned her head slowly. "Wow," she said. Zoe had even managed to make the top look fuller. Long bangs were sideswept across her forehead.

"Wait, wait! This is the finishing touch." Zoe leaned over and applied a light coat of mascara to Cara's stick-straight lashes and a dot of berry lip gloss. "Just a little. You don't want to look like you're trying too hard."

Cara got up from the chair slowly. "Zo, this is amazing. I never knew my hair could look like this."

Zoe beamed. "I know, right? You're just like Kristen Stewart." She bent over the magazine she'd been looking at when Cara came in and flipped the wrinkled pages. "There, see?"

Cara peered over her shoulder. Kristen was standing on a red carpet in a long navy silk dress, turned to one side, looking slightly uncomfortable. "Yeah, you're right." There was a vague resemblance between the actress's big dark eyes and delicate cheekbones and her own.

Zoe jumped up. "But the clothes . . ." She flung open Cara's closet.

Cara looked down at her faded bathrobe. "What about my clothes?"

"Cara." Zoe spoke patiently as if addressing someone with limited intelligence. "You can't go around with that awesome new haircut wearing a Mickey Mouse sweatshirt."

"I like that sweatshirt," Cara mumbled.

"I know," Zoe said soothingly. "It's a relic. But, Car, we have to do something about your clothes. Come on, don't you have anything else in here?" She pawed past three years of track T-shirts, a pilly black cotton turtleneck, four hooded cotton sweatshirts in various shades of gray. "You're a fan of variety, apparently." Zoe eyed the sweatshirts before pulling a clingy green top from the back. Tags dangled under the sleeve. "Ah-hah! What's this?"

Cara winced. "Oh God, that's nothing. Something Mom found on sale. She goes on these shopping rampages, trying to fix me up. I've never worn it."

Zoe tossed it into her lap. "You're wearing it now. And these." She held up Cara's best black ballet flats.

Cara hesitated and then yanked her sweatshirt over her head, mussing her new haircut. "I'm going to feel weird wearing this to school." Zoe tossed her a pair of dark skinny jeans, and she pulled them on. "What do you think?" The fabric of the shirt clung, outlining her chest and abdomen. The draped neck showed off her collarbone, which Cara always found embarrassingly prominent, like a coat hanger.

Zoe perused her, looking Cara up and down, as if she were a livestock buyer examining a prime steer at auction. Cara crossed her arms in front of her, oddly self-conscious. "Maybe if you stood up straighter, and kept your chin up more." She stood up and struck a pose in front of the mirror—shoulders thrown back, hands on her hips. She turned her head and eyed Cara coolly. "Come on, try it."

Cara got up from her stool reluctantly. She stood next to Zoe, her arms hanging limply at her sides. "I feel stupid," she said.

Zoe grabbed her arms as though they were strands of spaghetti and shook them. "Come on! Look, this will help you around Ethan. Now try it." She posed again, and Cara put her own hands on her hips, mimicking her.

"Shoulders back," Zoe instructed. "Now hips out a little more. *InStyle* says you can look five pounds lighter that way."

Cara arranged her body in the required posture. She looked at herself in the mirror. Zoe stood next to her, and for the first time, Cara realized they were exactly the same height and weight. With their dark hair and light eyes, they looked like two mirror images standing there.

"Okay, now repeat after me," Zoe said. "'Hi, Ethan.'" Her voice was airy and smooth.

"Hi, Ethan," Cara repeated obediently.

"No, no. Like you don't care," Zoe told her. "And keep your shoulders back. Like this." She demonstrated.

Cara straightened her spine. "Hi, Ethan." She tried a breezy little smile.

"That's better! Okay, now try this: 'Great meet yesterday.'"

Cara repeated her line. She raised her eyebrows at Zoe in the mirror hopefully.

Zoe furrowed her brow. "You're almost getting it. But something's not quite right. Here, say it with me: 'Hi, Ethan. Great meet yesterday.'"

Cara repeated the words along with Zoe.

"Again!" Zoe instructed.

Over and over, they said the sentence together, gazing into the mirror. Cara's voice blended with Zoe's until she couldn't tell whether she was speaking or Zoe was.

Chapter 9

T HE TRAINING ROOM WAS QUIET WHEN CARA PUSHED
open the door at six thirty the next morning.
She liked to get in early to stretch before everyone else arrived—it was a good time to decompress before
all the stress of the school day started. There was something
so relaxing about being in the little cinder block room alone,
with the heat blowing from the ceiling vents and the smell of
Pine-Sol from the janitor's cleaning the night before.

She hated to admit it, but a teeny part of her was happy
to have a few minutes completely to herself. She and Zoe had
been having a lot of fun, but she'd never shared her room
before, and it wasn't the hugest space in the world. She'd tried
to explain why she liked coming to the training room to Zoe
when she left the house half an hour earlier, but Zoe had just
squinted at her, looking hurt, before rolling over and pressing
her face into the pillow.

The small room seemed overly warm today. In fact, it was
like a freaking sauna, Cara thought, as she let the door swing
shut behind her. She dropped her gym bag on the bench and

examined the thermostat on the wall. Eighty-three degrees. Jesus. Like Saudi Arabia. She tried to dial it back, but the thing was impossible to move. What the hell? Was this some new sadistic training trick of Coach Sanders's?

Cara could already feel a trickle of sweat trailing down her back as she collapsed on one of the floor mats to stretch. She pulled her T-shirt over her head and pitched it in the direction of her bag, then stretched both legs out in front of her and bent toward her knees. The air felt odd flowing over the newly naked back of her neck. God, her hamstrings were tight this morning. She pressed her spine a little farther toward her legs.

She was going to debut her new look this morning, the green shirt and makeup tucked in her bag for after her shower. *Don't worry,* Zoe had told her before she had left. *No one's going to say anything mean. I just know.* And the funny thing was, Cara believed her. Zoe always just knew. Like when Cara's new kitten wouldn't stop peeing in the living room fireplace when she was eight. Her parents told her they'd have to give Tennessee away, and she sobbed for hours. But then Zoe told her that she shouldn't worry, that Tennessee would get to stay, she just knew it—and she was right. It turned out he simply didn't like his litter box. Once they got him a different kind, he was fine. Cara sighed and reached for her ankles. Well, Tenny was gone now. Replaced by fat, ugly Samson.

The training room door banged open. Cara looked up to see Ethan barreling in, a distracted look on his face. He stopped short when he saw her. "Oh, hi," he said. "I, ah, didn't know anyone else was here." A faint flush crept into his cheeks as his gaze traveled from her face down to her bare shoulders. Cara snatched up her T-shirt and pressed it to her chest. Her ears grew hot.

Ethan turned. "I can leave," he said. "I was just grabbing my spikes." He took them out of his locker and went over to the door.

"No, no!" Cara pulled her T-shirt over her head. She frantically searched for something to say, anything so he wouldn't leave. She took a deep breath. Now was the time.

"Great meet yesterday," she said, just as she'd practiced with Zoe, with the right mix of airiness and confidence. The fact that she'd gotten a sentence out around Ethan, something she'd seemed incapable of doing before, gave her the courage to go on. "Was that last runner killer in the relay, like Coach said?"

Ethan sat down on a bench nearby and leaned over, resting his forearms on his knees, the spikes dangling from his hands. His shoulders pushed at the fabric of his gray T-shirt.

"Yeah, he was tough," Ethan replied. "I remember that guy, actually. I think I ran against him last season, too. He used to go to Country Day."

"Guess he's just following you around," Cara said with a smirk. She didn't know what had come over her, but suddenly she wasn't feeling uncomfortable anymore. Maybe it was the thickness in the air, which had made her muscles loosen immediately. If only all of high school could take place in a sauna.

Ethan grinned and nodded. "Seriously. Too bad I beat him again." A rubber band was looped around one of his wrists, and Cara couldn't take her eyes off it. Ethan's face grew serious. "Hey, by the way, Sydney lived next door to you, right?"

"Yeah," she said slowly, wondering where he was going with this.

"Did you see her, you know, that night?"

Cara flashed on Sydney's laughing face, staggering around the pool. White jeans floating in the water. Part of her wanted to talk about what happened, but she didn't know how to tell Ethan what she'd seen without revealing she'd been watching the whole time. "No. I went to bed early."

He nodded. "I was just wondering. Alexis is really upset still."

Cara stiffened at the mention of Alexis, but Ethan didn't seem to notice. He was rummaging through his gym bag. Then he rose from the bench and tossed his spikes over his shoulder. "I've got to go finish some of that Euro History reading from yesterday. It's taking me forever."

"I know. Me too," Cara lied. She'd blown through it in about an hour last night, Zoe next to her on the bed, painting her toenails a violent green.

Ethan turned around again, his hand on the doorknob. "Nice talking with you, Cara. You're always so quiet at practice."

Cara could feel her face go scarlet. "Yeah, that's kind of my default state."

Ethan grinned. "See you later. By the way, your hair looks cute that way," he called over his shoulder as the door slowly closed behind him.

Cara fell back on the mats, her hands clasped over her hammering heart. She laid there for a good ten minutes, waiting for her body to recover. "Oh my God," she said to the ceiling tiles. An entire conversation with Ethan Gray—and he saw her in her sports bra—*and* he gave her *two* compliments.

Cara rose from the mat and made her way toward the showers on unsteady legs. Next Prince William was going to call from England and ask her to marry him.

Cara fluffed the back of her hair for the twentieth time as she stood in the doorway to the cafeteria. The noisy chatter rose from within. But instead of the usual sick feeling spreading through her stomach, she felt only the bubbly remnants of her encounter with Ethan that morning.

"Cute shirt, Cara," someone said behind her. She turned around to see Sarit standing behind her, holding something that looked like a long, foil-wrapped relay baton.

"Thanks!" Cara glowed and adjusted the clingy hem. Sarit was the third person who'd noticed her new look. In English, a girl she didn't know told her she liked her shoes. "Hey, um, what is that?" She pointed to the foil baton-thing.

"Oh." Sarit looked slightly embarrassed. "A dosa. It's like a giant pancake. My mom makes them. By the way, that was an awesome finish yesterday," she went on as they crossed the cafeteria. *Like actual friends.* Oh God, this was pitiful. But Cara couldn't help it. She knew her face was wearing a big sloppy grin.

"Oh, I didn't win," Cara pointed out. They turned into the food line, and she grabbed a tray from the stack, setting a peanut butter sandwich and an applesauce on it. Best to keep away from any foods she could choke on. That was the only thing that could ruin her winning streak today.

"Yeah, but that girl was a freakin' Amazon," Sarit countered. "We couldn't believe you had to go up against her. I swear she was either, like, twenty-five or on steroids." She pulled a bottle of iced tea from the cooler, and they walked toward the table. The other track girls were already seated, unwrapping their sandwiches and prying open Tupperwares. Julie had nothing in front of her except a giant-size Butterfinger. "New diet, Jules?" Sarit raised a dark eyebrow.

Cara had almost reached the table when someone bumped her shoulder hard and mumbled, "Oops." Cara stumbled forward, just managing to hang on to her tray. She turned around. It was Alexis, with Ethan by her side. Cara's stomach dropped, but Alexis barely seemed to recognize her. She just kept walking in a vague, unfocused sort of way, trailing the strong scent of coconut.

"Sorry, Cara," Ethan apologized. He hurried after Alexis, who had pulled out the chair at her usual table. She tried to sit down but only caught the edge of the seat, ending up in a messy heap on the floor.

"Ooh," Alexis moaned. "Shit."

Cara's eyes widened. She watched Ethan haul Alexis to her feet.

"Why don't you get Jack to carry you around?" Ethan growled. She tried to shove him, but he deposited her in the chair. She mumbled something indistinguishable and took a sip from a water bottle she was clutching.

"Oh my God," Sarit said. "Did you smell her?"

Cara nodded. "Yeah, like coconut." She set her tray down and took a seat next to Julie.

Sarit shook her head. "Like booze! She reeks of Malibu."

She unwrapped her dosa and took a bite. It smelled delicious, like potatoes and onions.

"We were sitting in American history, and all of a sudden, she just burst out in tears," Madeline said, spooning some mandarin oranges into her mouth. "Everyone just sat there until Mrs. Bolton told her to go wash her face."

Julie finally unwrapped her Butterfinger lunch and took a huge bite. "Basically, she's just been acting nuts ever since Sydney died," she said, blowing a shower of orange crumbs all over the table. "Sorry." She swallowed with difficulty. "She's going over the edge."

"Just like Sydney did," Sarit said. "I can't believe she just fell in the pool like that. Maybe she hit her head."

"Maybe she dove in," Madeline suggested. "Like remember that video they showed us in eighth grade with that guy diving into a pool and breaking his neck?"

Rachael shuddered. "The whole thing is so creepy and gross."

Everyone nodded in agreement. Cara bit into her peanut butter sandwich and thought of what her mother said the other day, about the police still investigating the case. *Investigating* . . . But a drunk girl drowning in her own pool hardly seemed worthy of a *Law & Order* episode.

Sarit nodded over toward Alexis's table, interrupting Cara's thoughts. "It's honestly just so sad. I mean, can you imagine if your best friend just up and *died*?"

Cara suddenly pictured finding Zoe dead, face down in a pool. Her throat almost closed up just thinking about it.

Her eyes slid over to Alexis's table. Alexis's head was cradled in her arms, and there wasn't any food in front of her, just the water bottle. Ethan was bent close, rubbing her back and talking to her softly. A strange feeling rushed over Cara, and it took a moment for her to identify it. *Wow. I can't believe I'm actually feeling* sorry *for Alexis Henning.*

Almost as if he'd heard her thoughts, Ethan looked over. Their eyes met. He gave her a sad little smile and nodded toward Alexis. Cara nodded back. She tuned back into the conversation around her. The girls were speculating on Coach Sanders's social life. Cara smiled and nodded at the right times. As soon as she got home, she'd tell Zoe about this—how they all just talked, like real friends. Cara finished her peanut butter sandwich and carefully brushed her new hair behind her ears. Her throat felt layered with sticky peanut butter. She took a swig from her water bottle. Actually, maybe she wouldn't tell Zoe. Zoe always got a little jealous whenever she thought Cara was replacing her. Cara swallowed again and again, but she couldn't get rid of the peanut butter coating her throat. It was choking her all over again.

Briefly, panic rose in her belly, but she fought it back and forced herself to drink the rest of her water. At last, the peanut butter washed away.

No, she decided, it was better not to tell Zoe. She wouldn't understand.

Chapter 10

"Zoe?" Cara called, cracking open the door of her
bedroom after school. She was panting a little from
her sprint home after the final bell. She couldn't wait
to tell Zoe about her encounter with Ethan in the training
room. "Zo?" The curtains were drawn against the gray afternoon, leaving the room in half-shadows. Cara softly shut the
door behind her.

The room was deserted, the bed tumbled with sheets and
sprawling pillows. A stack of magazines sat on the floor near
the nightstand, along with an empty plate. Cara's heart started
beating a little faster. "Zoe?" She looked around. Then, in an
instant, she knew, just *knew*, that this was the end. Zoe had
left, gone who knows where, leaving her to face her life alone.
Her breath whistled through her nostrils.

She heard a clink from the bathroom and rushed over to
the door. Zoe was there, standing at the counter, carefully
applying mascara. The rest of Cara's makeup—most of which
was years old—was spread out in front of her. Zoe looked
around. "Oh, hi," she said without smiling.

Cara sagged against the doorjamb, then made her way into the bathroom, where she collapsed on the closed lid of the toilet. "Oh my God, you scared me half to death! I thought you were gone."

Zoe applied a coral lipstick. "Nope," she replied, snapping the case closed sharply. "Still here." She bit the words off sharply, as if spitting out orange seeds.

"Well, don't do that again," Cara said. She took a deep breath and her heart slowed to its normal rhythm. "Anyway, you'll never believe what happened this morning—actually, this afternoon, too, but really this morning. Remember how I went in early to stretch? It was boiling in that room, so I—"

Zoe shoved the lipstick back in Cara's flowered makeup bag and whirled around. Her eyes were spidery with mascara. Her coral lips gleamed stickily. "Yeah, that's great, Car. I'm glad everything's going better at school, but you know, you might want to think about someone other than yourself for just one tiny second, okay?" She pushed past Cara into the bedroom.

"What are you talking about?" Cara stood uncertainly in the doorway. Zoe flung open her closet door and was rapidly sorting through the clothes.

"I *mean* ever since I got here, it's been Cara this and Cara that, and boo-hoo, my life is so awful, and Zoe, will you help me?" Her voice was hard. Zoe pulled out a short red dress with the tags still attached. "And I *have* helped you, even though you're oblivious."

"Zo, I'm sorry." Cara reached out to her friend, tears already pricking beneath her eyes. God, how could she have been so selfish? After everything Zoe had gone through with

78

her stepdad, this was the last place she should feel neglected.

Cara tried to put her arms around Zoe, but she drew away. Dropping her sweatpants to the floor, Zoe pulled the red dress over her head. Fear clutched at Cara's heart. There was nothing worse than having Zoe mad at her. It was the one thing she couldn't stand.

"You're right," Cara pleaded. "I've been so wrapped up in all my little problems, I haven't been thinking about you." She placed a tentative hand on her friend's back. This time, Zoe didn't move. "Can I do anything to make it up to you?"

Zoe whirled around and looked Cara in the face. "I want to go out."

Cara took a step back. "What? No! Zo, you can't. It's way too dangerous." She looked around the room. "Do you want some different food? I can go out and get us anything. Or a movie? Or . . . some books?"

"No." Zoe's face was dark. "I'm sick of being cooped up in here. Either you come with me or I'm going by myself. But I'm going out. You can't stop me, you know, Cara." She moved toward the door.

"Zoe, wait!" Cara clutched at her arm. "Your parents are probably looking for you. They might have even called the police. Please! I'd die if they took you away." Hysterical tears gathered in her eyes, threatening to overwhelm her. Cara's body shook at the thought of losing her friend again. Her face must have shown her anguish because Zoe's arm relaxed under Cara's hand.

"I'd die if they took me away too," she said. Slowly, she sank down on the bed.

Cara took a deep, shaky breath. "Okay," she said carefully.

"Just wait one second." She pulled two pairs of boots from the closet. "I've got the perfect solution."

Ten minutes later, they were tramping across an overgrown meadow behind Cara's house, rain jackets open against the light drizzle, the goldenrod brushing their calves above the boots. Zoe still wore the red dress, now damp with rain. She looked doubtful. "Cara, this isn't really what I had in mind." She glanced up at the gray sky.

Cara grabbed her hand and tugged. "Come on!" she said. "It's only across that next field." She pointed to a dark smudge of trees in the distance. "See that? It's in those woods."

"Where are we anyway?" Zoe pushed aside a tall clump of grass.

"Just an old farm," Cara said. "All these fields are overgrown. No one comes around here anymore. I think the guy who owns it checks in maybe once a year. But otherwise, it's just sitting here." The woods loomed in front of them. Cara pulled Zoe in among the rough trunks of the pine trees. "There." She stopped.

"Oh, wow." Zoe breathed. They were standing in front of a decaying barn. The boards that made up the walls were rotten at the bottom and broken off like jagged teeth. In a few places, peeling red paint was still visible, but the rest of the barn was a weathered silver gray. The roof sagged dangerously, almost swaybacked. A row of glassless windows gaped from the side like pits. "What is this place?"

Cara tugged at one of the big doors at the front. It slid open reluctantly, screeching on its rusted rails. She stepped into the dank, musty interior. "It's my hideout. I just like to

80

come down here sometimes to chill, read, you know, just get away from things." She gestured around her. The dust motes floated cheerfully in the air when it was sunny out, but today, the leaden sky pressed at the cracks in the walls. A steady *drip-drip* came from somewhere in the back.

On either side of them, old stalls had once held horses and perhaps a cow, but now the partitions were rotted, and some had crashed over entirely. Ancient straw reeking of mold was still spread on the floor. Here and there, rusted pieces of farm machinery sat like remnants of the Inquisition. A crude set of steps in the corner led to an open hayloft, which spread across the top half of the barn. Zoe looked up to the dizzying rafters, soaring fifty feet above them. A window was at each end, but no barn swallows soared in and out today.

Cara led Zoe to the farthest stall, where a rough gray blanket had been patted into a sort of nest. "Here's where I hang out," she said. "I've got a flashlight, a water bottle, a cushion. And . . ." She reached into a corner and pulled a cellophane bag out with a flourish. "Tortilla chips! I left them last time I was here."

Zoe smiled. "It would've been so fun to have a place like this when we were growing up." She sank down on the blanket and pulled open the bag of chips. Her dress was riding up on her legs, showing her grayish underwear, but Zoe didn't seem to care.

"I know! Remember all that time we spent behind your house?" Cara sat down.

"Making fairy nests?" Zoe grinned.

"Frog nests," Cara corrected her.

"Right, frog nests!" They both laughed. Cara remembered

81

the loamy, sour smell of the dirt and the way the stiff honeysuckle branches would poke her in the legs and back. She remembered the big brown bottles scattered in the dirt, "Colt 45" on the faded labels. She hadn't known what they were back then. "Colt" was like a horse, but why would someone name a drink after a horse?

"Remember when we found that old beer?" Cara asked Zoe. "And you drank some. I thought you were so bad!"

Zoe nodded. "I was such a messed-up little kid." She shook her head, smiling a little.

"Not like anything's changed!" Cara poked her friend playfully in the stomach. Zoe's face darkened and instantly, Cara knew that had been a mistake. Zoe's mouth tightened. She scraped intently at the dirt floor with a stick while Cara waited tensely. For her punishment. No—that just jumped into her head. Zoe was her friend. They could tease each other, just like they always had.

Zoe threw the stick down and, as if she'd come to a decision, rearranged herself on the blanket so she was facing Cara.

"So, what happened with Ethan this morning?" Her voice was friendly and relaxed. The tension of the previous moment was gone.

Cara exhaled. "Well," she said, wiggling into the proper position for a good talk. "I was in the training room, like I said, stretching out, and I'd taken off my shirt because it was so hot." She described Ethan's face when he came in, and how he blushed, and then she blushed. "And we actually, like, *talked*, for maybe five minutes. And he said I was funny. I think guys really like that in a girl, don't you think?"

Zoe nodded. "Totally. That's usually one of the things

they say is most important. That and big boobs." She stuffed another chip in her mouth.

Cara rolled her eyes. "Okay, I've got one out of two." She thought of the way his eyes crinkled up at the corners when he smiled. Unable to sit still all of a sudden, she jumped up from the blanket and cruised the perimeter of the stall, tracing the splintery old wood with her fingers. "Whatever. It doesn't matter. He'll never be with me—he's got Alexis."

She turned around. Zoe was watching her. She seemed to be considering something. "Do you think he'd go out with you if she wasn't in the picture?"

"Like if they broke up for real?" Cara snorted. "Zo, first of all, that'll never happen. They've been together since freshman year, and they break up all the time, but it never sticks. Second, Ethan's never going to make a move on me because I'm *me*. I mean, look at this." She spread her arms, indicating her stained navy hoodie and baggy, faded jeans.

"That's not true," Zoe said indignantly. "You're a thousand times nicer and cuter than Alexis Bitchmobile. He just hasn't realized it yet. But he will eventually—I know it."

Cara shrugged and collapsed on the gray blanket. "I'm happy for crumbs. I did get to talk with him alone."

Zoe blinked. "Wait. Was this the first time you'd actually been *alone* with a cute guy?"

Cara thought briefly about denying it—she knew how lame it was—but it was no good around Zoe. She nodded.

Zoe stretched her legs out in front of her and leaned back on her palms. "Okay, so be honest. Have you been out on a date yet? Even in a group?"

Cara shook her head. "No. Never. I've barely been to any

parties since high school started." She sighed and sank down in front of Zoe on her knees. "I know how lame that sounds."

Zoe smiled. "Whatever. You don't have to worry about sounding lame in front of me. But wait, I'm not done."

Cara sort of wished she'd drop this particular line of questioning, but Zoe was pinning her in place with the force of her violet eyes.

Zoe leaned forward. "Have you ever kissed a guy before?" Her voice was low and conspiratorial. Her breath smelled a little stale.

Cara shook her head. "No. See how screwed I am? I'm seventeen, and I've still never kissed anyone!"

"So how are you going to know what to do when you finally do kiss a guy?" Zoe raised her eyebrows.

"I don't know. Get a book out of the library?" Cara giggled nervously.

Zoe scooted a little closer. She hadn't shaved her legs in a while, and dark hairs sprinkled the white flesh of her thighs. "Well, you should practice," she said.

Cara barked a laugh. "Right. With a pillow? Or maybe Samson?"

"No, dumbass." Zoe playfully smacked her shoulder. "With me." She leaned forward and put both hands on Cara's blue-jeaned knees.

"What?" Cara wasn't sure she'd heard correctly.

"I'll practice kissing with you. That way, the next time the situation comes up, you'll be ready." Her eyes stared directly into Cara's.

Cara shifted a little on the gray blanket. She could feel the scratchy wool pricking her through her jeans. What Zoe was saying did make sense. She couldn't deny all the times she'd thought in panic that she was going to look like a total idiot when—*if*—some guy ever did want to kiss her, remote as that possibility seemed. "Well, okay," she said slowly.

Zoe grinned and arranged herself cross-legged so that she was facing Cara. Their knees almost touched. "Okay," Zoe said. "The first thing you want to do is close your eyes."

"Right." Cara closed her eyes. "I already knew that one." She stared at the darkness on the inside of her eyelids. She could hear Zoe rustle a little next to her.

"Then, you just part your lips a little, but don't purse them. You have to keep them soft."

Cara did as instructed. She felt kind of stupid, sitting there with her eyes closed in the middle of a barn, with her female best friend. But she didn't have much time to muse on it, because she felt Zoe's soft hands on her shoulders and sensed her leaning close. Without thinking, Cara started to open her eyes. She just caught a blurred glimpse of Zoe very close to her.

"Don't open your eyes!" Zoe barked. Cara obediently squeezed them shut again.

"Then you just want to press your lips very softly against his, like this," Zoe said. Cara felt Zoe's cheek brush hers and then Zoe's lips pressing against her own. After a second, Cara started to pull away, but Zoe's nails bit into Cara's shoulders. Her lips were insistent. Cara's eyes flew open, and she started in surprise. Zoe's eyes, ringed with smeared mascara, were staring right into her face.

Cara jerked away. "I thought you said to close your eyes."

Zoe smiled, apparently unruffled. "I said *you* should close your eyes. I didn't say anything about me. I was being the guy, and usually they don't close their eyes. They're weird like that."

Cara didn't say anything.

"You want to try it again?" Zoe asked. Without waiting for Cara to answer, she leaned forward and pressed her mouth against Cara's. For a brief instant, a wave of claustrophobia swept over Cara, as if the walls of the barn were closing in around them. The world was consumed by Zoe's closeness to her. She tried to pull back, but she felt strangely immobile. The grit on the barn floor pressed painfully into her knees. Then she felt Zoe's lips pressing harder against hers and then the tip of Zoe's tongue touched the tip of hers like an electric shock.

Cara choked and broke away from Zoe, scrambled to her feet. She stared down at her friend, who still knelt on the blanket, her hands on her bare knees, smiling placidly up at Cara. She glowed in the dimness of the barn as if lit from within.

"Well, what do you think?" Zoe asked. Her voice was calm and friendly, as if asking what Cara thought of a new movie. "Do you feel better now? You'll be totally prepared the next time you and Ethan are alone together, right?"

Cara didn't say anything. Zoe stared at her.

"Right, Cara?" she asked more insistently.

"Right," Cara heard herself whisper. Her voice sounded as if it were coming from a great distance.

Zoe nodded, satisfied by this answer. She rose to her feet and grabbed Cara's icy hand with her own warm one. "Come on, I'm freezing. Let's get out of here."

Cara let Zoe run her out of the barn into the rain. The

sky had darkened, and black clouds rolled overhead. Thunder boomed and a streak of lightning flashed across the eastern sky. Cara looked at Zoe, and they both screamed, then burst into laughter.

"Come on!" Zoe shouted over the wind. She grabbed Cara's hand, and they raced across the fields, stumbling, their wet hair tangled across their faces. "We're going to get soaked!" Zoe yelled, panting. Like a dream upon waking, Cara felt the memory of what had just happened recede, like the silent barn behind them, fading into the trees.

Chapter 11

"REMEMBER HER?" CARA POINTED. "SHE WOULD LICK the palms of her hands in class!"

Zoe's dark head bent over the fourth-grade yearbook spread across her lap. She squinted at the page. "Sort of. What was her name? Leila?"

"Leah. She always smelled like dried spit." Cara shuddered at the memory and flipped the page. She pulled the rumpled bedcovers farther up on her lap. It was four o'clock and she had yet to leave her room, except for a few turkey-sandwich forays. Behind them on the laptop, *On the Waterfront* played silently. Cara had wanted to prove to Zoe how much Ethan looked like a young Marlon Brando.

"Oooh, I hated fourth grade," Zoe said, stretching her arms over her head. "That was when I tried to run away that first time, remember? My stepdad got even worse after that."

"I remember." Cara shifted uncomfortably on the bed. That was when she'd started playing with Jill Westerfeld a lot. They'd do chalk drawings in Jill's driveway and see how far they could jump off her front porch. Zoe hadn't liked that very much. Or at all. Cara thought of her own panic when Zoe had screamed that she was leaving, since Cara didn't need her anymore—she had Jill. Cara had grabbed her friend's backpack off her back and fell down on the floor of Zoe's room, screaming and begging her to stay. They found Zoe hiding in a Dumpster outside of Wendy's by the highway, Zoe told her when she returned two days later. And her stepdad never let her forget it. Cara stopped going over to Jill's after that—chalk drawings and sleepovers weren't worth losing Zoe. Nothing was worth losing Zoe.

Now her friend slid onto the floor next to a stack of old magazines. She picked up a copy of *InStyle* and leafed through it. "Look, you could do this with your new cut." She held up the magazine, and Cara leaned forward to examine a model with a sleek, slicked-back style.

"That looks like a lot of gel," she said doubtfully. A knock came at the door. Cara's heart gave a huge leap in her chest, like a mouse trying to escape her rib cage. "Shit!"

Zoe slid into the bathroom, smooth as a snake. She closed the door soundlessly, just as Mom called, "Cara? Are you ready?"

Cara searched her brain for the event she was supposed to be ready for. She cracked the door. Mom stood there in a gray suit and gold earrings, Samson cradled in her arms. "What are you talking about?"

"Sydney's service." Mom looked slightly surprised. "Didn't you remember, Cara? We're leaving in ten minutes." She peered over Cara's shoulder. "Were you sleeping, honey?"

Cara resisted the urge to slam the door in her mother's face. That probably wouldn't go over well. She heard the bathroom shower curtain rustle, and the mouse in her chest gave another leap. She pasted on a pleasant smile. "No, I didn't forget. I'll be downstairs in five minutes. Just have to fix my hair."

Mom nodded, and after giving the room one last searching glance, trailed down the hall. Cara watched her until she went downstairs, then turned back into her room. "Damn it!" she cursed, flinging open her closet door. Zoe peeked into the room from the bathroom.

"Is she gone?"

"Yes," Cara said savagely, pulling a black jersey dress over her head. She grabbed a pair of pantyhose from her underwear drawer and stepped into them hastily.

Zoe sat on Cara's bed, hands clasped between her knees, watching. "Wow, you really don't want to go to Sydney's memorial, do you?" she observed. "Those hose are going to get runs if you yank them like that."

Cara forced herself to pull the black hose gently over her knees. "I'm just annoyed I have to spend all afternoon watching people cry over someone we all know was really a bitch. I'd rather have all my teeth pulled." She stopped short, her hand to her mouth. "Oh, wow. Sorry. That was really mean."

Zoe yawned. "Don't apologize to me—I'm glad the bitch is dead. Actually, it's nice to see you get a little bitchy. You're so nicey-nice usually." She flung herself back onto Cara's unmade bed and picked up *InStyle* again.

Cara took a swipe at her hair with her hairbrush. "It must be your influence." She sighed and set down the hairbrush. "I'm just pissy because I have to watch Alexis sob all over Ethan's shoulder for the next hour."

"Mmm, sounds great." Zoe wiggled luxuriously on the bed, crooking her arm over her face. "You go on and enjoy Sydney Sob-Fest 2011. I'll be here taking a nap on your bed." Cara pitched a flip-flop at her head. Zoe's laughter trailed her like a ribbon as she descended the stairs.

Outside, the afternoon sky was a deep, dazzling blue. A jet-trail traced a silver line far overhead. Cara shot a quick glance at Sydney's house, hulking next door like a sleeping giant. It was shut up tight, the shades drawn and the front door closed. The driveway was empty of cars. Sydney's parents had probably already gone to the church. Cara averted her eyes and hurried down the driveway.

Mom and Dad were already waiting in the Lexus with the engine running. Cara slid into the backseat. There was silence in the car as Dad backed down the driveway. Cara crossed her arms on her chest and stared out the window at the manicured houses sliding by. It wasn't that she hated Sydney or anything, she told herself. It was just that she'd already gone through this at the school assembly. Did she really have to say good-bye to Sydney twice when once was more than enough? *Bitchy, bitchy,* Zoe said in her head.

I'm not, Cara argued. *I just hate pretending.*

In the front, Dad cleared his throat. Cara looked up in time to catch a significant glance passing between her parents.

"What?" she asked, instantly on the alert.

Mom twisted around. Her red lips shone like a candy apple against her freshly powdered face. A faint furrow was outlined between her brows. She cleared her throat. "Well, sweetie, ah, Dad and I were wondering . . ." She stopped and nervously folded her lips.

Cara looked from one parent to the next. "What's going on?" Her heart clutched. They'd found some evidence of Zoe. A shirt left somewhere. Or worse—the police had called. They were closing in. She felt a sick sweat break out on her forehead.

Her father spoke from the driver's seat. "We just want to know if you're feeling all right these days, Cara. Your mother's noticed how pale you are."

"I feel fine," Cara replied warily. Was it a trap to get her to admit to hiding Zoe?

Her mother sighed and glanced at Dad again. He gave her a slight nod. She turned around again. "Honey, it's just that you've been spending an awful lot of time in your room this last week or so." Her blue eyes were wide and concerned. "Dad and I were wondering if you're under too much pressure at school. Maybe you should hold off on track until next year."

Cara slumped back against the seat, the tension flowing out of her like a river. She exhaled the breath she didn't realize she'd been holding. "Mom, no. God, is that all? I'm fine, okay? Track is great." She knew she was babbling slightly, but she didn't know where to stop. "Don't worry about school. I'm actually doing better than ever. I really like some of the kids I'm with this year." Her voice grew stronger.

Mom looked doubtful. "Are you sure?"

"Mom! I'm sure!" Cara struggled to keep the edge from her voice. "I'm positive," she said, more softly.

Her mother sighed and faced forward again. Dad patted her on the knee as he turned down a busy commercial street. Cara could see the yellow brick church up ahead, flanked on either side by a car dealership and a chili parlor. "I believe the service is expected to be quite large," Dad said.

"Poor girl," Mom said. "So young. It was awful seeing her lying there. I can't believe it happened right next door."

Dad pulled up in front of the church, a squat, flat-roofed building surrounded by an ugly parking lot. A few anemic shrubs straggled near the front. A plain black sign reading SECOND METHODIST was carved over the glass doors. The place looked more like a bank than a house of worship. "I'll never get a parking space," Dad said. "Marge, I'll drop you two off. Maybe there're some places around back."

Cara and her mother climbed from the car, the brisk wind blowing around their legs. Cara held her dress down with both hands. Well-dressed people in overcoats and suits were standing in clusters on the step, chatting. Cara spotted Sarit in a group of their classmates. She smiled and nodded, but Sarit either didn't see her or didn't want to see her. Cara let her mother steer her by the elbow through the crowds into the overheated vestibule of the church.

The church bell rang once, and people began filing inside. The air in the vestibule quickly took on the smell of damp wool. The babble of people around her was low but unceasing. Cara felt the noise worming its way down her ear passages and into her brain, where it lodged above her forehead like a swarm of bees. She let the crowd carry her into the large, airy sanctuary, decorated with stained-glass windows in abstract designs. No gory crucifixes for the Methodists—the only cross in the whole place was a modest, light-wood structure over the altar in front.

Cara spotted Sarit, Julie, and the others crowding into a

back pew. Alexis limped up the aisle with her friends surrounding her as if she were a grieving widow and was inserted into a side pew halfway from the front. Ethan was nowhere to be seen. Sydney's parents were visible as stick figures sitting stiffly in the middle of the front pew. A large photo of Sydney in a low-cut black dress—Cara recognized it as cropped from last year's Prom Court portrait—sat on an easel at the front, flanked by large sprays of purple delphiniums.

Dad hurried up the aisle, and Mom nudged Cara into a nearby pew. She obediently slid in with her parents on each side. Their presence seemed to close in on her. A bland-looking young man with spectacles stood up from his chair at the side of the altar and opened a large black binder. He was clearly the minister, though he wore an ordinary suit and tie. The crowd grew respectfully quiet.

One of the doors at the back opened. Cara turned to see Ethan, looking impossibly handsome in khakis and a crisp blue shirt, his hair still damp from the shower, hurrying up the aisle. A little murmur ran through the crowd as he slid into the pew next to Alexis and put his arm around her. She pressed her damp face into his shoulder.

The minister began. "Dear friends and family, today we are gathered to remember a special young woman, someone who left us too soon."

Cara wiggled in her seat, trying to get comfortable on the hard wood, while the minister buzzed on about Sydney's lust for life, as he put it, her love for her parents, friends, school, the world. A parade of relatives and classmates appeared on the podium and disappeared. Lips mouthed words of sadness, mourning, remembrances of Sydney on the football field sidelines, at family holiday parties, stocking the local food pantry for World Hunger Day. Cara could feel her legs going numb as the edge of the pew cut into the bottom of her thighs. A draft curled around her ankles. She glanced over at her mother and caught her surreptitiously checking her Black-Berry. Mom looked up guiltily and slid the phone into the open handbag at her feet.

"Let us pray." The minister bowed his head. Cara stared at the bitten nails pressed together in her lap. The cuticles were ragged, and the backs of her hands were rough. She really had to start using hand cream.

"Amen." The minister looked up. Everyone stood and began gathering purses and jackets, talking to one another in low voices. Several groups filtered up to the front and embraced Sydney's parents.

Cara stood up, knees cracking, and stretched her back.

"Well, now, wasn't that nice?" Mom sounded like she was on auto-parent.

"Very nice," Dad echoed.

Cara mouthed Mom's next words along with her. "I wonder if I have time to stop by the office for a bit."

Cara nodded. "I'm sure you do, Mom." Might as well release her as soon as possible. Cara followed her father's charcoal gray–clad back up the aisle, stopping every foot or so as people moved slowly out of the pews and back into the vestibule.

The noise level increased, as if the congregation had just been let out of class. Cara left her parents making polite conversation with Madeline Brazelton's parents and made straight for the water fountain in the corner. She pressed the shiny metal bar, drinking deeply until her thirst was slaked. Cara wiped her dripping chin on the back of her hand and turned around, smacking into someone standing in line directly behind her.

"Oh God, sorry!" Cara blurted. It was Sarit, wearing a gray sweater dress and a pair of tall, tight brown boots.

She grinned. "It's okay. This place is so hot. I'm dying of thirst." She bent over the water fountain and slurped, while Cara stood there like an idiot, wondering if she should walk away, or wait.

Sarit straightened up. She blinked when she saw Cara still by her side, but regained her composure quickly. "So, wasn't that service, like, so sad?" she said as they crossed the lobby. The place had emptied out quite a bit. Cara's parents were still deep in conversation with the Brazeltons, while a few groups of kids still hung around talking.

Cara nodded her head, perhaps a bit too emphatically. "*So* sad," she echoed. They had almost reached the group of track girls standing near the doors. Cara had a flash of her old anxiety—was she supposed to stand and talk with them? Or was Sarit just chatting with her on the way over to them?

She stood at Sarit's side briefly as they joined the group, feeling intensely awkward. After a minute of standing there with an idiotically casual smile pasted on her face, with no one talking to her still, she crossed the lobby to her parents, and stood near them like the world's most useless appendage. They didn't even acknowledge her presence, they were so immersed in their conversation with the Brazeltons— something about property taxes. This might just cap her status as the biggest loser in the world, Cara thought. Her own *parents* weren't even talking to her.

The track girls were trailing out the door. Then Sarit said something to them and broke off from the group. Cara watched in disbelief as Sarit crossed the now-empty lobby toward her.

"Hey, Cara, a few people are coming over to my place to hang out and, you know, like, remember Sydney," she said. "You want to come?"

Mom broke off her conversation finally and looked over. "Sarit Kohli?" she asked. Sarit nodded. "Goodness, I hardly recognized you! You girls are getting so big."

Sarit smiled patiently.

"Thanks, Sarit, that would be great," Cara jumped in before her mother could humiliate her any further. She tried to control the big sloppy grin that threatened to take over her face.

"Oh, yes, that would be great!" Mom echoed. She gave Cara a little push. "Have a good time, honey." She waved as if Cara were going off to a kindergarten play group.

Sarit grinned, and Cara rolled her eyes as they hurried across the lobby and outside. Madeline's red Mazda was idling at the curb. Julie was in the front, while Rachael and another girl Cara didn't know were stuffed in the back. Sarit climbed in next to them and after a moment's hesitation, Cara followed.

"Hey, Cara," Julie greeted her.

"Sarit, get off my leg," Rachael said.

"There's no room." Sarit laughed. Cara scanned the car for signs of irritation that she was horning in, but no one looked annoyed. In fact, no one even seemed surprised that she was there. Cara relaxed against the door, squished as she was, and Madeline pulled into traffic. It was only after they were several miles away that Cara thought about Zoe—alone in her room, waiting for her to come back.

Chapter 12

*S*ARIT'S DOORBELL RANG OVER AND OVER, AND THE large sunken living room quickly filled up with kids from school. People streamed in and slouched onto the couches and floor. Bob Marley played quietly on the stereo in the corner. Cara perched at the edge of a couch, her purse feeling like a suitcase in her hands. A giant bowl of pretzels appeared and slowly made its way around the room. People talked in low voices, with only the occasional burst of laughter. A purple dusk was beginning to gather outside the large picture windows.

Cara looked around for Sarit, but she couldn't see her or any of the other track girls. They were probably in the kitchen. Through some sliding doors on the right, a group of kids perched on lounge chairs drawn up around a fire pit. She recognized Alexis's figure, lying against the back of a chair. She looked like she was asleep. Jack was sitting next to her. Ethan was out there too, on Alexis's other side, poking at the fire with a long stick. His eyes were focused on the dancing flames, and Cara wondered if he was deliberately trying not to look at Jack or Alexis.

She forced herself to smile at a tall guy next to her. He was wearing a blue tie pulled down, with his collar unbuttoned. She didn't really know anyone—they were mostly seniors. Two girls across from her looked over with blank eyes. One of them took a pretzel and nibbled at it daintily. Cara's hands felt as big as hams. She placed them next to her on the couch, but that felt weird, so she folded them in her lap, which felt even weirder.

"Where's Sammi?" a tall dark-haired girl sitting on the floor asked.

"You know," the guy with the blue tie replied meaningfully. Everyone burst out laughing at Sammi's unnamed whereabouts, and Cara tried to laugh too. She felt like there was a giant POSEUR sign plastered to her forehead.

"What was she thinking?" The tall girl sighed.

Her friend rolled her eyes. "What is she always thinking? She knew they'd be gone."

"But they weren't!" A blond girl laughed. More merriment. Cara could feel her smile grow more fixed. She willed her eye not to start twitching, but God help her, it did. Of course. The twitch began slow and small but quickly increased until she could feel the edge of her eyelid almost vibrating with it.

Cara got up quickly, catching her toe on the edge of the coffee table and stumbling a little. "Sorry," she mumbled to the group. She thought she could feel their eyes following her across the room.

The cluttered kitchen was deserted. Dishes crowded the sink. The window over the sink looked out onto the small backyard, with an old wooden garage at the back and a neighbor's picket fence beyond. Cara poked around in the cabinets for a clean glass and finally pulled down a coffee mug reading

SHERMAN HIGH JUNIOR PROM COURT, 2005. QUEEN was embla-zoned on the handle. Must have been Sarit's older sister.

Cara took a deep breath, relaxing for a moment in the unobserved quiet of the room and felt her eyelid twitching slow and then stop. She ran water into the mug and took a sip. It was warm and metallic-tasting. As she dumped it out she gazed at her reflection in the darkening window. Her face stared back at her, the eyes wide and dark. Her hair fell loosely around her face. The shadows under her eyes were deep gray smudges. Then, over her shoulder, she saw Ethan come into the kitchen.

She whirled around. His tie was loosened, and his hair was rumpled, as if he'd run his hand through it a few times. "Hey there." He smiled in his easy way. "I didn't know you were here."

Cara's throat closed up, but she managed to say, "Yeah, I am." *Brilliant, Cara. Would you like fries with that?*

Ethan opened the fridge and studied the contents criti-cally. He extracted a bottle of iced tea and opened a nearby cabinet. It was full of pots and pans.

"Oh! Here." Cara handed him a 2005 Prom Court King mug that matched her own.

"Thanks. You want some?"

"Uh, sure." Cara handed him her mug and watched as he filled it halfway, then poured the rest into his own.

He handed her the mug, and the tips of his fingers grazed hers. Her hand shook.

"Whoops. Don't drop it." He smiled at her, and for one second his light blue eyes looked right into hers. Cara thought she might go into cardiac arrest right then, but she forced herself to take a firmer grasp on her mug.

Ethan leaned back against the counter and gulped half his tea. "The funeral party. It's such a weird thing to do, don't you think?"

Cara smiled a little. "Yeah, I know. But I guess nobody really wants to be alone right now." She cast a glance through the open doorway into the crowded living room. "I don't really know a lot of people here."

Ethan shook his head. "Me neither. I hate parties, actually."

"You?" Cara couldn't help exclaiming. "You always seem so . . ." She cast around for the word. "Social," she finished lamely.

Ethan raised his eyebrows a little. "Yeah? That's funny. Usually I feel like I just move around in this little bubble of friends. I hardly hang out with anyone except our group, and Alexis . . ." His voice trailed off. He cleared his throat.

Cara shifted her weight. She was suddenly aware of how close they were standing. "Why do you hate parties?"

Ethan drained the rest of his tea. "Probably because I used to be fat." His voice was muffled and his face half-hidden by the uptilted mug.

"What?" Cara wasn't sure she'd heard him right—or if he was kidding.

He lowered the mug. A crooked little smile touched his mouth. "You didn't know I was the fat kid in middle school?"

Cara shook her head.

"Dude, I was huge!" Ethan dug in his back pocket for his wallet. He flipped it open and pulled a creased photo from behind his driver's license. Cara studied it. A much younger, much chubbier Ethan stood awkwardly in front of the Grand

Canyon, surrounded by his family, everyone squinting into the sun.

"You weren't so bad." She handed the photo back, and he tucked it away again.

"I used to wear my dad's shirts to hide my gut." Ethan tapped his fingers on the counter. His ears were pink. "Anyway, I was like the loneliest kid in the fifth grade. I literally had no friends." His voice had a veneer of carelessness.

Sympathy flooded Cara's heart. She wanted to take his hand, hanging by his side, and squeeze it. "But then everything turned out all right," she said instead. She could hardly believe *she* was comforting *Ethan*.

Ethan grinned. "Yeah. I grew like six inches when I was eleven. But still, every time I see some little fat kid on the street, I want to go up and tell him, 'It's going to be okay, buddy. You'll get through it.'" He put his mug and Cara's in the sink, and together they walked out into the packed living room.

"And he'll be wondering, 'Who is this crazy guy, and what the hell is he talking about?'" Cara replied, laughing.

Just then, someone behind her said, "Bitch"—very loudly, very clearly.

Cara turned, her laughter dying in her throat. Alexis was standing in the doorway leading to the patio, vodka fumes hanging around her in a cloud. Maren and another girl stood behind her, along with Jack. Their eyes were shiny with interest, like theatergoers getting ready for the show. Alexis wavered, steadying herself with a hand on the doorjamb. Her hair was mussed up at the back and flattened on one side, and her mascara was smudged.

"What the hell are you doing here?" she spat, her eyes

narrowed. The venom in her voice drove Cara back against the couch arm. "You didn't even know Sydney. She hated you, you loser." The living room full of people grew quiet. There was no sound, except for the occasional clink of ice in a glass.

"We used to laugh at you all the time, did you know that?" Alexis was slurring some of her words. She stumbled, almost losing her balance, and caught herself. "Sydney always said you were the best entertainment at Sherman, *Choker*." She lingered over the word, drawing it out.

Cara could feel the roomful of avid, shiny eyes fixed on her back. She wanted to run away but couldn't. Her eyes felt locked onto Alexis's twisted face. Her eyes were terribly bloodshot, and the rims were puffy. Her skin looked dull and pasty. "You're such a creep, Cara. Sydney knew that about you. You're so pitiful. And now she's dead and you're not."

Alexis brought her face so close, Cara could see a vein throbbing in the middle of her forehead. "It should have been you in that swimming pool, Cara. It should have been you that night—not Sydney. It should have been you." She was screaming now. Spit sprayed from her lips onto Cara's forehead. Cara's body began an uncontrollable trembling.

"Alexis! Shut up!" Ethan grabbed her by the arm and hauled her back a few steps. He gripped her shoulders. "You're drunk. Go lie down. You're being a total bitch."

"Why don't *you* shut up, Ethan." Jack stepped forward from the doorway. The crowd gasped.

Ethan glanced at Jack, his face hard. "Stay out of this." He tried to steer Alexis out of the room, but she shook off his arm.

"Get off me!" she screamed. "What are you doing, defending this loser? Fuck off, Ethan!" Her voice was terrible, like a buzz saw in the quiet. Ethan dropped back a step, his arms by his sides, and Alexis whirled around with a sob and ran from the room. The front door slammed.

The silence in the house was thick. Cara tried to swallow, but the lump in her throat was still huge. Blindly, she turned away from the crowd, stumbled back into the kitchen, and bent over the sink, gripping the cold metal edge with her sweaty palms. She willed herself not to be sick. Behind her, she could hear faint murmurs beginning.

She stared out the window over the sink. The yard glowed in the night, brightly lit by floodlights. Then Cara blinked. She thought she saw movement near the back, like someone slipping behind the garage. She could have sworn she saw the flutter of long black hair. But before she could think about it anymore, Ethan's warm hand touched her back.

"You okay?" he asked. Cara looked into his face. His icy blue eyes were concerned. She nodded shakily and pulled out a chair at the kitchen table. She couldn't look at Ethan. Did he agree with those things Alexis said? Did he think she was a creep and a loser?

The party was over. People started gathering jackets and bags and trickling out the door. No one said much. Outside, cars started up. The living room was a depressing shambles of spilled drinks and mashed cups. Sarit was already trailing around with a large garbage bag, picking up.

Cara could feel the tears slowly running down the sides of her nose. She knew her face was getting all blotchy and swollen. Suddenly a wad of fresh, soft tissues appeared in front of her. She looked up. Ethan was holding them out.

"Come on," he said. "I'll walk you home."

Chapter 13

HE NIGHT AIR WAS COOL AND STILL. A HUGE orange harvest moon hung in the eastern sky. Cara walked next to Ethan in silence, her hands stuffed into her parka pockets. Their footsteps made soft, scuffing noises in the leaves that had fallen on the sidewalk. When had that happened? Fall had come without Cara even noticing. The last she remembered, the leaves were still green on the trees.

Ethan's shoulder bumped hers slightly. "Sorry," he apologized.

"It's okay," she whispered huskily. She wasn't entirely sure she wasn't going to start crying again.

They tromped past the neat brick houses lined up along the street like sentinels. Each lawn was a perfect square, dark green and silvery with early frost. The street was empty and dark except for the yellow glow of one streetlamp at the end. Cara imagined she could hear the echo of their footsteps bouncing off the houses they passed.

Ethan was silent, his hands in his coat pockets. Cara

wondered if he was mad. At her? At the whole situation? Finally, she couldn't stand the silence any longer.

"Ethan—" Her voice sounded faint and trembly in the still night air. Cara realized she'd never said his name out loud to him before. It tasted foreign in her mouth. She stopped. She didn't know what to say after that.

"Cara, I'm sorry," Ethan said. "That whole thing was my fault."

"What?" she asked. "How could it be your fault?"

He shook his head. "I saw how drunk she was getting. I should have taken her home then." He paused. "I just get tired of dealing with her moods—especially lately." He glanced over at her. "I feel like a jerk for saying that."

"No!" Cara reassured him. "It must be hard to take care of someone during a time like this." She glanced up at his face as they walked. His profile was outlined against the moonlight. A brisk breeze ruffled her hair, and Cara shivered involuntarily. Ethan glanced down.

"Are you cold?"

She shook her head, but he took a pair of heavy fleece gloves from his pocket and handed them to her. She drew them on. They were way too big, but warm. She resisted the urge to rub them against her face.

"Yeah, Alexis can be kind of hard to get along with sometimes." A wry smile twisted the corners of his mouth. "I don't know if you'd noticed that."

Cara giggled. "A little."

They walked in silence for a while, but it wasn't awkward anymore.

"Can I tell you something?" Cara said after a minute.

Ethan nodded. His eyes were calm.

Cara took a deep breath. "It's just something that's been on my mind for a while." She paused. Ethan waited. "It's just that—well, I heard from my mom that Sydney's death . . . may not have been totally an accident." She felt the weight of the secret ease a little just saying it aloud.

Ethan's brows creased. "What do you mean?"

Cara shook her head. "That's all I know."

"Like, someone pushed her or something?" Ethan stopped walking.

"I don't know!" The words came out louder than Cara intended. She lowered her voice. "Seriously. It's just freaking me out thinking that Sydney could have taken her own life, or even that someone else could have been involved . . ." She hadn't let herself entertain that thought before, but saying it aloud made it seem like a real possibility. Could someone have wanted Sydney dead?

Ethan put his arm around her shoulder and squeezed. "It's okay. Look, don't worry." He dropped his arm and started walking again. "They're probably just trying to be really thorough."

"Yeah." Cara focused instead on how it had felt to have Ethan's arm around her, and she let herself be comforted.

They passed through a little "downtown" section—a bakery, a shoe repair, an architect's office, a dentist, the windows all darkened. The police station, brightly lit, the squad cars pulled up out front like a row of shiny bullets. An older woman came toward them with a golden retriever on a leash and passed quickly, the dog straining to sniff their legs.

"Can I ask you something?" Ethan said.

Cara nodded.

"Why are you so quiet at school?"

She paused. Had he been watching her at school? All that time she thought he was totally consumed by Alexis. She realized he was waiting for an answer. But how do you answer a question like that? "Well, I'm actually a deaf-mute by day. Like being a vampire but not as fun."

Ethan snorted, and she grinned at him and rolled her eyes.

"Okay, I get the hint," he said. "I won't ask nosy questions."

"No, no. It's okay." Cara resisted the urge to cross her arms over her chest like a shield. She sighed. "I just feel out of place. It's actually kind of like what you were talking about before, how you felt in middle school. Except it's still happening to me. Like I think people are watching me, but I don't know how to act or what to say. It just seems easier to stay out of the way." She couldn't believe she was just spilling her guts like this. But it was like the soft night had transformed her into someone else. She laughed a little.

"What?" Ethan smiled a little.

Cara shook her head. "Nothing. It's just that I've never said that out loud to anyone before. I've never even admitted it to myself, I don't think. But I don't know, things have been different recently. I've gotten . . . back in touch with this old friend, Zoe— she was my best friend until we moved here. Anyway, she's one of those people that can make you act crazy. You know them?" Up ahead, she could see her house, the porch light glowing, at the end of the block. Her parents' cars were in the driveway.

Ethan laughed. "Yeah, I've definitely known a few of them." His hand swung down and brushed hers. The shock of his skin warmed her right to her bones.

"This is my house."

"Nice," Ethan said. "Now that I know where you live, I can come harass you whenever I want." He grinned.

"Definitely." Did Ethan Gray really just suggest he was going to come over sometime? Could this really be happening? Maybe someone had slipped something into her drink at Sarit's, and she was hallucinating. If so, it was the best hallucination of all time.

He stood at the foot of the driveway, hands stuffed in his pockets, waiting until she had unlocked the front door. She turned and waved before she went in, then shut the door.

Inside, the house was dark and still. Her parents were probably in bed. Cara floated up the stairs. She hoped Zoe was still up. She couldn't wait to tell her about tonight. The Ethan part, not the Alexis part. Funny how one night could be so great, and so terrible, all at once.

Reaching her room, Cara opened the door softly, in case Zoe was already in bed. The lights were off, but even in the dim light from the hall Cara could see the wrinkled sheets. The bed was empty.

"Honey, I'm home!" Cara called softly. She shut the bedroom door behind her and looked around. "Zoe?" Cara went over to the bathroom, already anticipating Zoe's figure standing at the cluttered sink. But the bathroom was deserted too, the pink polka-dotted shower curtain pushed to one side. Cara knelt and pressed her hand on the bath mat, which lay wrinkled on the floor. It was damp.

"Zoe?" Cara said again. No answer. Cara stood in the middle of the room, looking around, the panic rising in her belly. "Zoe?" Her voice quavered, like a lost little girl's in the dark.

Cara sat on the edge of the bed and took a deep breath. Maybe she was overreacting. After all, Zoe had said she was getting antsy. Maybe she just went out to the barn. A little wave of relief rushed through her at the thought. That was it. She'd gotten bored and was hanging out in the barn for a little change of pace. She'd probably be home before Cara had even fallen asleep.

She flicked on the bathroom light and squirted some makeup remover on a cotton ball. She rubbed it over her eyelids. Zoe's disappearance was vaguely irritating—after all, she'd told her how dangerous it was for her to go out. But on the other hand, at least it was nighttime. Hopefully, Zoe had the sense to stay in the barn and not go anywhere she might be seen.

Cara dropped the black-smeared cotton ball into the wastebasket and stuck her toothbrush under the tap. She examined her face in the mirror as she brushed, expecting herself to look different somehow. This was the face of someone who'd walked home with Ethan Gray. And they'd really connected—she just felt it.

Cara bared her teeth, toothpaste foaming around her mouth. White and straight, thanks to three years of braces. She turned her head slowly right and left. Normally, she avoided mirrors. But tonight she looked almost pretty. Her new short hair fluffed out around her face, and her cheeks were flushed from excitement and the cold. Her eyes were wide open and sparkling. She could almost, *almost* imagine that she was a girl Ethan would find attractive.

Cara rinsed her toothbrush and hit the light, plunging the bathroom into darkness. Shedding her wrinkled black dress,

112

she threw herself across her bed and pulled the soft old cotton comforter around her shoulders. As delicious sleep overtook her, she hoped that Zoe, wherever she was, was being careful.

Cara was dreaming. Ten-year-old Zoe's face floated in front of her. Her long black hair was held back by a headband, showing her high white forehead. She held up a can with a blue drawing of a rodent on the front, and Cara felt an odd mix of excitement and dread in her belly. She knew what was going to happen, but she couldn't stop it. She had to watch until the dream was over.

Cara looked down at herself. She was wearing the denim shorts and yellow T-shirt that had been her favorite in fifth grade. The leather sandals she wore endlessly that year were on her feet, the right buckle broken, as it always had been. All around her, Zoe's backyard in the old neighborhood spread out in Technicolor. The grass was eye-poppingly green, and the sky overhead glowed the blue of sapphires. In pantomime, Zoe waggled the can in front of Cara's eyes. Cara felt her head nod, even though inside she was screaming, "Wait!"

Slowly, she and Zoe walked over to the broken-down chain-link fence. The neighbor's German shepherd was chained today. He lunged for them, straining against his collar, barking furiously and silently. Cara's dream-self ran her hand over the bandage on her arm. She remembered the blood gushing from the bite wound, and all of a sudden, a hot, glad fury filled her heart. She watched Zoe shake the poisonous blue crystals into a can of dog food. They gleamed on the wet brown surface like rare jewels. Zoe stirred the crystals with a stick, then held the can out to Cara. Her face was horribly eager. Cara watched her hand go out and take the can. She shoved it through the bottom of the fence and crouched down next to Zoe. The dog, immediately distracted, hunched over, chewing and licking until nothing remained but the shiny-clean can.

Zoe grabbed Cara's arm and pointed. Already the dog's hindquarters were quivering. The girls watched, squatting, their arms wrapped around their knees, as the tremors spread upward along his spine to his forelegs, then his head. He reeled across the yard as if his legs were no longer his own, then snapped back against his chain and fell with a thud to the grass. His mouth hung open. Foam drooled from his tongue. His legs peddled helplessly at earth, tearing away chunks of grass.

Zoe stared at the dog, her face alight. Cara stared at Zoe.

She awoke suddenly with a gasp and sat up in bed, her nightshirt drenched in sweat. She looked at the bedside clock. 3:47 a.m. With a trembling sigh, Cara slowly lay back down on her pillow. It was the old dream. She hadn't thought about the dog in years. But after the poisoning, she'd had the same nightmare for weeks.

Cara folded her arm over her eyes, trying to slow her hammering heart, and only then did she realize that someone was in bed beside her. She jerked convulsively, biting back a scream before she realized that it was only Zoe. Of course. Her friend lay curled on her side, eyes shut. She was deeply asleep. Cara propped herself on one elbow and gazed down at her. Zoe's old gray T-shirt was a little sweaty, and her breath was whistling fast through her nose. Cara could hear the little whine as her friend inhaled and exhaled. Her eyes twitched like live animals, and her fingers grasped at the sheets, then relaxed.

She turned her head from side to side as her lips mouthed an unintelligible word. Cara had the disturbing sensation that Zoe was dreaming about the dog too. Her friend's legs twitched and shuddered, just as the dog's had when he died. Then Zoe's breathing slowed. Her fingers relaxed. She sighed, turned on her side, and was still.

Cara watched her for a second longer. Then she dragged her pillow to the very edge of the bed. Curling herself into a little ball, facing away from Zoe, she squeezed her eyes shut and willed herself to sleep. But she laid there for a long time, awake behind her closed eyelids, before deep sleep finally reached up and dragged her back down.

Chapter 14

CARA OPENED HER EYES TO CLEAR SUNLIGHT STREAMING in her window. She glanced over at the other side of the bed, half-expecting to see Zoe gone again. But she was there, the top of her dark, glossy head only barely visible under the covers. Quietly, Cara slipped from under the warm nest of blankets and shivered as the cool dry air assaulted her sleep-warmed skin. She pulled on a hooded sweatshirt and stuck her feet into her sheepskin slippers, then ducked out of the room. Her parents' door was still tightly shut.

Downstairs, the kitchen was stuffy. Samson strolled in, mewing when he heard her, but Cara ignored him and cracked a few windows. She sniffed appreciatively at the damp leaf smell. High puffy clouds were scudding fast across the deep blue sky. She stuck a couple pieces of bread in the toaster, humming a little to herself. Just then, the back door slammed and Mom came in, wearing her running clothes, her face pink from the outdoors. She jumped when she saw Cara.

"Oh, honey!" she said. "I didn't know you were up."

Why did Mom always seem so surprised to find her in her own home? Like finding a houseguest who's stayed too long. "Yeah, I'm up."

Samson mewed more insistently. Mom scooped him up. "Baby! Cara, you didn't feed him?" She took a can of salmon dinner from the pantry and started cranking it open. The fishy smell made Cara want to hang her head out the window.

Mom measured coffee into the coffeemaker. Cara drummed her fingers on the counter. The silence stretched out.

"Oh! I almost forgot! How was the get-together last night? Sarit is very sweet." Mom bumped into Cara on her way to the fridge.

"It was fine, Mom. Sarit's nice." The toaster dinged. Cara grabbed a plate from the cupboard, and pulled the toast out, slapping on thick layers of butter and jam.

Mom took a sip of her coffee. "Cara, I asked Cheryl to clean your room when she comes today. She's going to shampoo the rugs, so pick up all your clothes so she can do yours, too."

Cara whirled around. "Mom, no!" Her voice was louder than she intended.

Her mother looked taken aback. "Why not, Cara?" she asked carefully.

Cara realized she was squeezing the plate so hard her knuckles were white. She relaxed her grasp. "It's just that I hate strangers in my room, touching my stuff. You know that."

"Well, honey, it's just Cheryl. And if you pick up your clothes, she won't have to touch any of your stuff, right?" Mom chuckled at her own joke and patted Cara's leg, but Cara jerked away without answering and pounded up the stairs.

"Room service." She pushed open her bedroom door.

"Ooohh." Zoe extracted an arm from beneath the covers and threw it over her eyes. "What time is it? Why is it so bright in here?" She tried to pull the covers over her head. Cara grabbed them and yanked them off. Zoe screamed and curled up like a shrimp in a T-shirt and gym shorts. "You're so awful! This is torture." She tried to grab the covers back, but Cara held them out of her reach and handed her a piece of toast instead.

"Get up!" she instructed. "Mom's having the housecleaner come in here today." She gathered an armful of dirty running socks and musty-smelling blue jeans and dumped them into the hamper. "So we have to get out of here. We're going for a hike—I know this great trail no one goes on—and a picnic at the barn." She crammed some of her own toast in her mouth. She was ravenous.

"Oh God, you're insane." Zoe propped her head in her hands. "Why do I feel like I have a hangover when I haven't even been drinking?"

Cara threw another sweatshirt and a pair of jeans in her lap. They landed on the toast. "Ooooh!" Zoe held up the jeans, the toast glued jam-side onto the butt. Both girls burst out laughing.

The only tricky part of the adventure was slipping Zoe down the stairs while Mom was in the shower. She kept giggling while Cara frantically shushed her. Once they were outside, things were easier. It was only a short, fast walk behind the houses—they couldn't use the sidewalk of course, much too

119

risky—and then they were safe behind the old elementary school, now boarded up.

"This trail starts right behind the water tower and ends near the barn. No one's ever on it." Cara hoisted her backpack a little higher on her shoulders. She didn't think a block of cheese, a box of Triscuits, and half a pepperoni would weigh so much, but the pack seemed to be getting heavier by the minute. She peered through the trees as they skirted the woods. A thin path wove through the dark tree trunks. "Here it is."

The girls plunged into the woods, pushing through a heavy thicket of blackberry brambles. In the summer, when the cicadas buzzed in the trees, these bushes were laden with huge, deep purple fruit. The air would be hazy with golden pollen, the sun a flat, blinding white disk in the sky. But now the brambles drooped dispiritedly, their branches a gnarled mass of stiff, brown twigs. The mud squished under Cara's boots, smelling of peat and rotting leaves. Ahead of them, the path curled up the hill, winding around fallen trees. Cara picked her way through the stream that ran at the bottom of the hill, watching the water wash up over the soles of her boots.

Zoe was quiet behind her. Something about the silence helped Cara broach the question that had been on her mind the last few days.

"So . . . have you heard any news from home?" She kept her voice casual.

"What do you mean?" Zoe answered after a second. She sounded a little out of breath.

Cara skirted a large mud puddle. "Nothing. I was just

120

thinking that your mom must be freaking out by now. I mean, it's been over a week."

Zoe snorted. "Not likely. I mean, she's probably freaking out, but not about me going missing."

"What do you mean? What's she freaking out over?" Cara turned to face her friend. Zoe's face was hard, her eyes blank.

"I did something bad, Cara. But it's not anything worse than what he did to me. Okay? I can't go back. And I don't want to talk about it." Without waiting for an answer, she pushed by Cara on the path and strode ahead.

Cara's stomach did a little flip. "Zoe, what are you talking about exactly? What did you do?"

Zoe stopped but did not turn around. "I think I just said I didn't want to talk about it." Her back was perfectly straight.

"Okay, okay," Cara soothed. Zoe started walking again. Cara tried to drag her thoughts back to the more immediate problem. She wasn't going to be able to keep her parents out of her room forever. It wasn't that she wanted Zoe to leave—not at all—but she needed to think of *something*.

She took a deep breath. "Zo. Whatever happened, we need to figure out—"

"So how was last night?" Zoe cut her off.

"Amazing. But listen, I've been thinking about this situation—"

"Where were you? I was waiting for you."

Cara gave up. The path was muddier than she expected, and she had to concentrate on not slipping. Better to wait until Zoe was in a more receptive mood.

"Yeah, I went over to Sarit's." She watched Zoe's back for signs of annoyance. "I had a really good time hanging out with Ethan. Alexis was a bitch again, though." She briefly described the living room encounter.

Ahead of her, Zoe's back was perfectly straight. Cara wondered how she managed to look like a runway model in a stained sweatshirt and Cara's too-big jeans. "See, the problem with you, Cara, is that you're letting her just push you around. You should've shoved her into a wall." She splashed right through a big puddle.

"Zo, your feet are going to be soaked!" Cara pointed out. She hitched up the backpack again. "And when have I ever shoved anything, anywhere?"

Zoe kept walking, even though her jeans were soaked to her knees. "Maybe that's why you've been such a loser in high school."

The words stabbed Cara like a knife. She stopped walking. "Wait—you think I'm a loser?" Even saying the word hurt. Once again, she felt the spray of Alexis's spittle on her forehead.

Zoe turned around. She sighed in an exasperated manner, as if talking to a difficult toddler. "Car. I didn't mean *I* think you're a loser. I'm just saying what *you* said everyone thinks."

"Oh."

Zoe started walking again, and Cara followed. She could feel twin blisters forming on the insides of her big toes.

A small rise loomed ahead of the girls. Cara began the uphill climb, the muscles in her calves straining. A lot of good all that running had done if she was going to be sore after a two-mile hike. The woods crowded around them, the damp branches reaching out to grasp at their shoulders. Cara's boots squished on the thick coating of wet leaves that covered the forest floor. After a few steps, she realized she could no longer hear Zoe behind her. She turned around. Her friend was standing halfway up the hill, gazing at something in her hands. "What?" Cara called back. Zoe didn't answer.

Cara tramped back down the hill, trying to keep from skidding in the deep mud. "What?"

"It was just moving around on the leaves, squeaking," Zoe said mournfully. She looked down at the tiny gray field mouse cradled in her palms. The mouse lay motionless. "It was suffering."

It took Cara a minute to absorb the situation. "Wait, you just saw this mouse on the leaves and picked it up?"

Zoe nodded. "I had to put it out of its misery." She looked up sadly.

For a minute, Cara didn't understand what she meant. "Jesus, Zoe, did you kill it?" The mouse lay limply, its neck bent at an unnatural angle, the long gray whiskers and little pink feet resting against Zoe's palm.

"Oh my God!" Cara exclaimed in revulsion. She reached out and swiped the mouse from Zoe's hand. It fell with a little thud to the leaf-covered ground. "That's totally disgusting." She stared at her friend. Zoe just gazed back, her violet eyes as calm as always.

Zoe shrugged and walked ahead of Cara. "So, do you think Ethan will want a big wedding, or is he the kind of guy who wants something small?" she called back over her shoulder. Cara stood still a moment, gazing at the little gray corpse at her feet, and then, on impulse, bent down and swept a handful of wet leaves over the body. It didn't seem right somehow just to leave it exposed to the elements.

"Come on, Cara!" Zoe called. Cara looked up to see her friend standing at the top of the hill, her figure outlined against the sky, now clouded with a scrim of white. Zoe's hair fluttered out in the breeze like a banner. "I'm beating you!"

They reached the barn a few minutes later. Cara heaved back the big doors, and Zoe immediately flung herself down on the musty hay. Cara felt slightly nauseous thinking of the dead mouse and stripped off her sweatshirt, fanning some air under her blue tank top. The moldy smell was more pungent than ever. The old boards of the stall creaked as Cara leaned back against them and rearranged the wool blanket under her legs. A flash of white up in a far corner of the rafters caught her gaze—an old cloth or something. The shadows were too deep to make out what it was.

Cara hauled out the food and dipped her hand into the crackers. For a while, they ate in silence. Then Cara stuffed the cheese wrapping and the empty Triscuit box back into her backpack, and Zoe closed her eyes. Zoe lay back down on the hay and tucked her hands behind her head.

Cara tipped the last few drops of water from her Nalgene and eyed her friend. "So, where were you last night when I came in?"

Zoe shifted slightly on the hay but didn't open her eyes. "Nowhere. I was bored, so I came down here to hang out. I fell asleep for a while, I think."

Cara cleared her throat. "So, you didn't go . . . anywhere else?" She thought again of the flash of long black hair behind Sarit's garage. Zoe wouldn't have followed her, would she?

Zoe sat up. "I just said I was here." Her face was blank, her eyes wide.

Cara fiddled with some strands of hay, arranging them in a square. "It—it's just that I thought I saw you . . ." Her voice trailed off. Zoe stared at her unblinking, running her fingers through her long hair. She pulled a few strands in front of her face and examined them for split ends. A brisk wind blew outside, rattling the panes of glass in the broken windows.

"Never mind," Cara finished lamely. She swept away the hay square with one palm. Zoe rolled something between her fingers.

"What's that?" Cara peered at it. It was a small pearl, almost glowing in the gloomy light.

"This?" Zoe held it up and examined it as if she were a jeweler. "Just something from my mom. Took it before I left." She suddenly sat up on her knees and peered through the window.

"Isn't this fun?" she said, turning to Cara with a big smile. "It's just like old times." She reached over to hug Cara. Her bare arms were soft. The faint scent of underarms wafted to Cara's nose. "So did Ethan try anything last night?"

Cara resisted the urge to push her away. "No, of course not. He's with Alexis! He's too much of a gentleman to do anything like that."

"I bet she won't be a problem anymore." Zoe laughed. Her teeth were slightly yellowed, as if she hadn't brushed them in a while. "Are you sure you didn't get a chance to use your practice lessons? Come on, tell me."

Her breath smelled awful. Cara casually shifted back a few inches. "No, nothing like that, I swear. You know I'd tell you right away if anything happened." God, it was awful that Zoe was letting herself go like this. Maybe she was depressed just staying in the bedroom all the time, never having any excuse to get dressed up. Cara put her hand on Zoe's. "Zo . . . I wish you could just come to school with me, and hang out, like normal. I hate that you're trapped in my room all the time."

Zoe looked surprised. "I don't."

Cara blinked. "You don't?"

"Nope. Why would I want to go to school? I have everything I need in your room . . . food, stuff to read, music—and you!" Her lips were stretched back from her teeth in a rictus-like parody of a grin.

Cara cut her eyes away. "Come on," she said suddenly, getting to her feet and hoisting the backpack onto her shoulders. "Let's get out of here. I'm freezing."

Zoe leaped to her feet, all trace of her earlier sluggishness gone. She pranced out of the barn and did a little skip, like a wood sprite, among the sodden golden grasses. Cara followed her dancing form up the hill toward home.

Chapter 15

A FTER THEY RETURNED FROM THE HIKE, CARA WENT INTO the bathroom and slowly stripped off her clothes. In one slow movement, her hand went out and turned the lock on the door. She didn't let herself think about why. Instead, she turned on the hot water and let the steam fill the tiny room. Her shoulders slumped, and her feet felt heavy. She climbed into the shower, noting the deep scratches up both legs and on her forearms. The brambles must have been sharper than she thought. The scratches stung as the soap cascaded over them.

Cara stood under the shower a long time, until the hot water turned tepid. She started to shiver again, but she didn't want to get out. She wanted to stay hidden in the tiny bathroom forever. At last, when the gooseflesh was pimpling her arms, she shut the water off and wrapped herself in her warmest bathrobe. She pulled on a pair of wool socks and her slippers and wrung the water out of her hair. But she couldn't stop shivering, not even after she aimed the blow-dryer at her face.

When she finally crept from the bathroom, the room was

dark gray with early-evening shadows. Zoe was facedown on the bed, fast asleep, still wearing her dirty jeans and boots. Cara tiptoed over and stared down at her friend. Dirt and bits of leaves littered the sheet, Cara noted with a faint sense of disgust. She could've at least taken off her boots. Her breathing was deep and regular. Zoe should rest, Cara told herself. She slipped on some clothes and snuck out of the room with a faint sense of guilty relief.

Downstairs, the house blazed with light. The gas fireplace was lit, and Dad was just coming in the door with a fragrant pizza box. Cara inhaled deeply. Her mouth was watering. Mom came into the living room with plates and napkins. Oh my God, she'd even made a salad. Cara resisted the urge to make a snarky remark about Betty Crocker night. "That looks amazing," she said instead. "Anyone else want a Diet Coke?"

Her father shook his head. "We're fine, thanks."

Cara grabbed a frosty can from the kitchen and threw herself on the living room sofa, loading her plate with three slices of pizza. The lamps glowed against the tightly drawn curtains, and the TV chattered in the background. Cara took a giant bite of hot cheese and dough, closing her eyes as she chewed. Even Samson wasn't mewing for once. He sat in his place on top of the couch, licking his side before lying down and staring into the fire.

Dad picked up the remote and flipped through the channels as Cara started on her second slice. It was amazing how hungry she was just from walking around in the woods. She reminded herself to set aside enough pizza for Zoe. Dad stopped at the local news.

"—the Eagles were down by three at halftime," the blond anchor was saying. Cara wondered if her orangey tan was on purpose or if something went wrong in the makeup room.

"Up next, a girl missing from Sherman High School. Did she run away? Police are investigating."

Cara sat up. The anchor disappeared, replaced by a dancing toilet brush. Cara set the pizza slice down on her plate and wiped her fingers with a napkin, concentrating on one finger at a time. The grease left translucent yellow spots on the white paper. Nothing ever happened in their little community—but first Sydney, and now this. Who could be missing? Maybe it was the goth girl who sat next to her in calc. She never, ever talked, not even when she was called on, and spent the whole class drawing pictures of bleeding daggers in her notebook. It was probably her—she seemed like the type to run away.

With this reassuring thought, Cara swallowed the bite of pizza she was chewing, tilted her can of soda up, and took a long slurp.

"Alexis Henning was reported missing last night after failing to return from a local party," the anchor's voice returned.

Cara spilled Diet Coke all over her lap.

Mom gasped. "Alexis? How terrible." She stared at the screen. Dad was riveted too, his slice of pizza forgotten in his hand.

On the TV, a portly, balding man stood on the lawn in front of a massive white-clapboard house a few miles away that Cara recognized as Alexis's. The man wore a green Windbreaker. A reporter who looked about twelve stood next to him. "Harold Salazar is Alexis Henning's uncle and the spokesperson for the family." He turned to the man. "Mr.

Salazar, what would you like the public to know about this situation?"

Alexis's uncle looked nervous. He kept looking first at the reporter, then at the camera. "This is a very distressing time for our family," he said, reading from a sweaty piece of paper clutched in his hands. "Alexis's parents ask that the media please respect their need for privacy in this distressing time"—Cara could see him realizing he'd repeated "distressing time"—"and anyone who has any information that could help find Alexis, would they please contact the police immediately. Thank you." He dropped his paper and disappeared below the camera's eye as he searched for it.

Cara's lips were cold. She barely noticed the dampness from the spilled Coke seeping through her jeans. The orange-colored anchor was back on the screen, now wearing a somber expression. A little thumbnail picture of Alexis floated to the right of her head. "Authorities suspect suicide in the case of Alexis Henning's disappearance," the anchor intoned. "She has been distraught since the death of her best friend, Sydney Powers." Alexis's picture disappeared, replaced by one of Sydney. Cara cringed as she recognized it as the same one used at Sydney's funeral.

The anchor went on. "Friends report that Alexis argued with her boyfriend soon before disappearing. Police are currently dredging Deer Fork River for her body." A video of the river appeared. The sky was overcast, and rain spotted the camera lens. Police in bright yellow slickers circled the river in power boats, while a small crane attached to another boat worked up and down. Cara thought she spotted Alexis's parents to the extreme right of the camera shot, clutching each

130

other on the riverbank. She imagined she could hear Alexis's mother sobbing.

"Oh, how terrible." Mom was pale. She set her plate down on the coffee table. "Poor Kathy and Mike. I'll call them in the morning. And so soon after Sydney's death! Perhaps she ran away. A suicide would be just too terrible to think about." She turned to Cara, still sitting motionless on the couch. "Had you heard that Alexis was missing, Cara?"

An image of Alexis's purple-glossed lips taunting her in the lobby flashed through Cara's mind. Alexis screaming at her at Sarit's, her face twisted into a grimace of rage. Cara's stomach roiled. She suddenly regretted that last slice of pepperoni. She shook her head. "No. I hadn't heard," she choked out.

Dad had gone back to his pizza. "Tragedy," he managed to say through his mouthful of cheese. He shook his head.

The nausea clawed its way up her throat. "Ooh," she moaned a little, shifting on the sofa. Mom looked over at her, sudden alarm in her eyes.

"Cara?" she asked sharply. "Are you feeling sick?"

No. It upset them when she was sick like this. *Say "no."* She shook her head, sweat beading her forehead. She couldn't even look at the greasy, cold pizza still sitting on the coffee table. She could feel it coming and bolted up the stairs to her room, leaving her parents in silence behind her.

Zoe sat up in bed as Cara burst through the door and into the bathroom. She collapsed on her knees in front of the toilet and hung her head over the bowl. The floor tiles were cold under her knees. She waited.

Vaguely, she heard rustling in the bedroom, and then Zoe's feet with their chipped red nail polish appeared near

131

her head. The soles were filthy from their walk earlier in the day. Cara could feel Zoe gazing down at her.

"What is it?" Her voice sounded detachedly curious, as if examining an interesting scientific discovery.

Cara retched once, but nothing came up. She waited a minute more, panting, but her stomach slowly settled back. Cara lifted her head and reached for a tissue. "Alexis is missing. They think she might have committed suicide." The words sounded surreal coming out of her mouth.

Zoe didn't even blink. She shrugged. "Yeah. She was totally falling apart. What a nut job." She turned, padding back to her lair of a bed.

Cara struggled to her feet and filled a cup with water at the sink. She drank some. Then she set the cup down and came to the doorway. Zoe was lying back on the bed, holding a copy of *Ferdinand the Bull* over her head. "I used to love this story," she said dreamily.

"Wait, how did you know Alexis was falling apart?" Cara asked.

Zoe looked over. "You told me. Duh."

"Oh, right, duh," Cara echoed.

"Here." Zoe handed her the book and patted the bed by her side. "Read to me."

Cara sat down on the rumpled sheets, and Zoe pressed up against her like a child. She closed her eyes and laid her head on Cara's shoulder.

"'Once upon a time in Spain,'" Cara began. She read and read as darkness fell outside the windows.

Chapter 16

CARA WAS DROWNING. SOMETHING WAS HOLDING HER down, and she couldn't get away. She fought through cottony layers of sleep and forced her eyes open. The yellow numbers on her clock read 5:30. Zoe was curled up right against her, her arm draped over Cara's. Her eyes were still closed, and she breathed with her mouth open. Cara winced at her stale breath. Zoe opened her eyes and looked right into Cara's. She smiled.

"Good morning," she said. She didn't move. Cara tried to smile back. She edged an inch away from Zoe, teetering at the edge of the bed, then slid from under the covers and felt around on the floor for her slippers.

Zoe flopped an arm lazily across the bed and grabbed Cara's vacated pillow. She stuffed it under her own cheek and, lying on her side, stared at Cara with her huge, sleep-ringed eyes. "What are you doing? It's so early."

Cara's skin was still crawling from finding Zoe so close to her. She stuffed a T-shirt and her spikes into her running duffel. "I think I should get to the training room early this morning.

I've been feeling really tight recently." She slid her history text and two binders into her backpack and zipped it up.

Zoe's face crumpled. "I thought we would have breakfast together this morning. I mean, I know I can't cook it or anything, but I had a special surprise planned for you." She rubbed a knuckle across her eyes like a little kid.

Guilt flooded Cara. Zoe was her best friend, and here she was, running away from her like she was some sort of pariah. She knelt beside the bed. "I'm sorry. What was the surprise?"

Zoe sat up. "I thought you could get us a breakfast sandwich somewhere and bring it back. Wouldn't that be fun?"

Cara blinked. "Oh. Um . . ." It's not like she was expecting Zoe to produce a full pancake breakfast from under the table, but an Egg McMuffin that *she* had to drive out and get didn't exactly sound like a special surprise. "I don't really have time this morning. Maybe tomorrow?"

Zoe's face closed down. She turned her back and shrugged. "Maybe." She propped herself up on her elbow and reached for the magazine on the nightstand. Cara stood behind her uncertainly.

"I thought you had to go," Zoe said without looking around.

"I do," Cara said. She laid a tentative hand on Zoe's back. "Hey, should I bring back some cookies from the bakery after school?"

Zoe shrugged her hand off. "If you want, Choker."

Cara stood there for another long moment. Her hands and feet felt cold. "What did you call me?" she finally managed to say.

Zoe glanced up, a little smile curling the edges of her lips.

For a minute, she looked like she was going to deny saying anything, but then her face changed. "Take a joke, can't you, Cara?" She pronounced Cara's name with exquisite care.

Cara forced a smile. "Of course I can."

Zoe nodded and looked back at her magazine. After a long moment, Cara turned and trailed slowly out of the room, closing the door behind her.

Outside, a white fog hung in the gray early dawn. The outside of the Volvo was pearled with dew, but the heater warmed up fast, and Cara drove down the quiet streets with the hot air blasting her feet. She mulled over the news about Alexis as she slid through the deserted intersections. It seemed weird that she would end her own life so suddenly. Cara always thought people who committed suicide had some sort of plan worked out. But maybe she'd just run away, like Mom said. She turned onto Springfield Pike. The bakery, Frieda's, had just opened, and a worker was sliding a tray of doughnuts into the window. On impulse, Cara turned into a parking space and killed the engine.

The inside of the tiny shop was warm and filled with the aroma of hot sugar. Cara inhaled as if she were taking a magic elixir. The woman behind the counter had neat gray dreadlocks and wore a wide smile. "Help you?"

"Can I get four glazed doughnuts, two chocolate, and two jelly?" She watched as the woman dropped the pastries into the bag. She'd take them back to Zoe this afternoon to make up for leaving her. *I'm just going to school!* a voice in her head argued. *Not exactly a crime.* Back in the car, she tucked the white paper bag into her duffel, nestling it in the middle of her clothes where it wouldn't get squashed.

The school parking lot was mostly empty when she arrived—a few lone cars scattered near the entrance, like dogs waiting for their owners to return. Cara hurried through the empty, freshly waxed halls to the training room. She pushed open the door, and froze.

Ethan sat hunched on a bench. His back was facing her, and his head was cradled in his hands, his elbows resting on his knees. His back was moving up and down a little. At first, she thought he was panting. Then he raised his head at the sound of her entrance, and she saw with a jolt that his face was streaked with tears.

"Oh! God, I'm sorry. I didn't know anyone was in here." Cara turned to leave.

"No, it's okay." His voice was a little thick.

Cara stopped with her hand on the doorknob.

Ethan swiped an arm across his face. "I was just—hiding out, I guess." He stared down at the floor again.

Cara edged forward. Hesitantly, she perched on the edge of the wooden bench next to him. He didn't move, just continued staring at the floor. Cara reached out and placed a tentative hand on his back, feeling the warmth under his shirt. He lifted his head, and she jerked her hand back as if she'd been burned. But his face was grateful.

"I saw the news," Cara said. "It's awful."

Ethan shook his head. The words poured out of him like someone had turned on a tap. "It's all my fault. I never should have gotten mad at her at the party. I should have known better. She's been so upset recently—so fragile. I'm such a fucking idiot." He smacked his knee with his open hand.

"Hey, don't." Cara bent down and tried to get him to look

136

at her. "Don't blame yourself. You—you were just doing what you thought was best."

He looked at her for the first time. His eyes were bloodshot and swimming with tears. "I just feel so guilty," he almost whispered. He reached out and clutched at her hand.

"I'm so sorry." She squeezed his hand back, and before she realized what was happening, his arms were around her and his head was pressed into her shoulder. She patted his back over and over as he cried. Cara could feel the heat of his body and the muscle and bone of his arms as they circled her. She felt very awake, as if she'd been given some sort of hyper-vision. She noticed everything—a tiny hole in the shoulder of Ethan's gray T-shirt, a flattened wad of gum on the linoleum at her feet, the yellow varnished surface of the bench, as hard and shiny as a butterscotch candy.

His tears had soaked the collar of her shirt by the time his sobs quieted. He pulled away, his cheeks pink. "Christ." He bent down and wiped his face with the hem of his shirt. "You must think I'm a total whack job."

"No! Of course not," Cara reassured him. He smiled a little, then cleared his throat. Cara stared down at her knees. Her shoulder burned where he'd rested his face. Silence fell. They sat next to each other on the bench as if at church.

On impulse, Cara reached down and pulled the little white bag out of her duffel. She stuck her hand in and found one of the glazed doughnuts. It was still warm. "Doughnut?"

He stared at it as if he'd never seen one before, and for an instant, Cara wondered if he was insulted. Maybe it wasn't the right time. Maybe he hated doughnuts. Maybe he and Alexis used to always get doughnuts together, and this was going to remind him of how awful he felt all over again.

Then his face cracked into a big smile. "Thanks. Wow. Yeah, a doughnut would be great." He looked at her wonderingly as he ate it in three big bites. Cara nibbled on a chocolate one. Ethan dipped into the bag again and started on a jelly doughnut. For a while, they chewed companionably.

Then Ethan swallowed his last bite and wiped sugar crumbs from his lips with the back of his hand. "My parents told me I didn't have to come to school today. But just sitting at home in my room would be a hundred times worse."

Cara nodded. "Yeah, I know about sitting at home." She folded the tissue paper in her lap into a square and smoothed it on her knee. "Actually, I kind of know what you're going through."

"You do?"

Cara nodded. "Yeah. I had to leave my best friend behind when we moved here. She was, like, the person I cared about most in the world. It was awful. I cried for days." Her throat swelled suddenly as she thought of Zoe back at home. Thank God Zoe had come back. All the tension of the last couple of days didn't matter. She was just lucky to have her friend back.

Ethan nodded. "Like, you just feel abandoned, right? One minute the person's right there, and the next, they're gone."

"You think about all the stupid fights you've ever had—"

"—and you wish you could take back everything mean you said." Ethan's mouth was drawn into a sad bow. "I lose my temper sometimes, like the other night at the party. Alexis always used to tell me to watch myself."

"Me too." Cara licked the sugar from her sticky fingertips. "I just get so *mad* sometimes. I let things get away from me, but I never mean it. It makes you feel powerless over your own emotions."

Ethan solemnly held up the last chocolate doughnut. "Sugar. The answer is sugar. Cures anything."

Cara grinned. "Coach is going to love it that we're OD-ing on disgusting carbs *and* getting crumbs all over his precious training room."

Ethan broke the doughnut in two and handed one half to Cara. "Good. I'm feeling a little rebellious right now."

She smiled and nodded, her mouth crammed with the sweet dough, happiness flowing through her veins. Sugar really did cure everything, after all.

Chapter 17

"ANY NEWS FROM SCHOOL?" MOM TOOK A BITE OF deli potato salad on Monday night and fixed her daughter with a stare.

Cara shook her head and maneuvered green beans from the three-bean salad around on her plate. Her father was forking in tuna fish with one hand while he made some sort of notes on a napkin with his other. Cara could tell he didn't even know what he was eating.

Her mother smiled patiently. Cara sighed. "Um, Mr. Furlong gave vodka to some of the football players at his house and got fired." There. That ought to keep her quiet for a while.

There was a pause as her mother digested this bit of news. Cara ate another bean. Her father said, "Hrumph!" at the napkin and nodded his head.

"Don." Her mother gave him a deliberate "this-is-quality-time-with-our-daughter" look.

"What?" Dad looked up. "What were you saying, Cara?" His eyes wandered to his plate. "Is that tuna salad?"

"She was saying that—" Mom was interrupted by the doorbell.

"I'll get it!" Cara slid off her seat. Behind her she could hear her mother continue recounting the Mr. Furlong vodka story. She had the daring, exciting thought that it might be Ethan at the door. She hadn't seen him since their training room encounter on Friday morning. But maybe he was stopping by to talk or something. With a tremulous smile on her lips, she swung open the door.

Two police officers stood on the doormat, under the porch light. Behind them, the dark autumn night hung still and chilly. Cara's heart gave a single huge thud, and she fell back a step. This was it, her mind buzzed. They'd found out where Zoe was. They were going to take her away, back to her stepfather. Cara wanted to run up the stairs and warn Zoe, but some calmer, wiser instinct held her in place.

"Is this the Lange household?" the female cop asked. She had neat blond hair pulled into a bun. Her name tag read "Stanton."

Cara nodded mutely.

"Who is it, Cara?" her mother called out from the kitchen. Cara's mouth was too dry to answer.

"May we come in?" the tall male cop asked. His badge glittered on his chest, reflecting the porch light. It shone right into Cara's eyes. She remained motionless. The cops, used to this sort of behavior perhaps, stepped over the doorsill anyway, forcing Cara to step back or get knocked over.

"Cara, who—?" Mom stopped in the entrance to the foyer, her napkin still in her hand. The faint look of annoyance on her face froze when she saw the police standing there instead of a Girl Scout selling cookies.

"Mrs. Lange?" Stanton asked.

Mom's hand flew to her throat. "Yes? Is anything the matter?"

Dad appeared behind her, his face startled. He placed a hand on Mom's shoulder.

"There is an urgent matter we need to discuss with you," the tall cop said. Cara looked at his name badge. Fitzgerald.

Cara felt the three-bean salad rise in her throat. This was it. It was all going to come out now. Zoe. Her concealment. Aiding and abetting a runaway. Was that a crime? Zoe hauled down the stairs, screaming and kicking. Would they handcuff her? Zoe crying out to Cara, holding her arms out. The cops, stone-faced, forcing her into the cruiser. Taking her away forever.

Cara made a strangled noise, and all four adults looked at her. "Cara," her mother said sharply. "Do you need to go get a glass of water? You're very pale."

Cara shook her head. Mom looked apologetically at the cops. "My daughter is a bit . . . nervous." Cara could see Mom gaining her composure back, going into lawyer mode. "Please, won't you sit down?" She indicated two matching armchairs.

The cops sat down, holding their hats on their knees, feet planted on the floor, backs straight, as if they'd been taught how to sit at the police academy. Mom and Dad sat together on the sofa facing them, while Cara remained standing, her back to the fireplace, her hands clasped behind her, like a child called up before the class.

Fitzgerald took a notebook from his pocket and flipped it open, poising his pen. "We're investigating the disappearance of a Sherman High School student, Alexis Henning. Are you aware that Ms. Henning was reported missing on Saturday, September twentieth?"

Cara felt the band of tension loosen from around her chest. It wasn't about Zoe. Zoe was safe. She felt like lying down on the floor. *But why are they asking me about Alexis?*

"Oh, yes," Mom said. "We saw it on the news. So terrible. We know her parents well. Is there anything we can do to help?"

"As a matter of fact, there is," Stanton said. She had a low voice tinged with a faint Boston accent. "We've found a pearl necklace that Alexis's parents have identified as hers. The necklace was found between the Kohli residence, where Alexis was last seen, and the Henning home. Neighbors have also reported hearing sounds of a scuffle. We've now shifted the investigation from suicide to a possible abduction." Stanton's face was smooth and blank. Cara flashed to the barn. Zoe rolling that little bead of light between her fingers.

"Abduction!" Mom gasped. Her hand went to her mouth. "Oh, poor Alexis!" Cara could see tears fill her eyes. She looked so old all of a sudden, sitting there on the sofa, her ankles crossed, her crisp white shirt gleaming in the lamplight. Cara could see every wrinkle on her face, every gray hair.

Fitzgerald cleared his throat. "We'd like to ask Cara a few questions, if you don't mind."

Cara could feel her ears grow hot as all four pairs of eyes swung toward her. Her eye began to twitch as if on cue. "M-me?" she stammered. From upstairs, she heard a door

144

open quietly. Zoe had come out of the room. Cara willed her face not to betray anything. From her position in front of the fireplace, she could see through the big open doorway to the staircase. A small white face appeared behind the balustrade. Zoe was watching them. Cara locked eyes with her for a moment, and Zoe winked. Cara thanked God that her parents and the officers were facing away from the stairs. But all Mom had to do was lean left a little, and look up and she'd have a direct view—

"Cara?"

"Huh?" Everyone was looking at her.

"Cara, Officer Stanton was asking if you could confirm you were at Sarit's on Saturday." Her father was looking at her strangely. "Pay attention. This is important."

"Oh!" Cara tore her eyes away from Zoe on the staircase. "Um, yeah, I mean, yes, I was at the party after the funeral," she stammered. Her eye was twitching a million miles a minute.

Fitzgerald made a note on his pad. "And while you were there, did you happen to speak to Ethan Gray?"

Ethan? She nodded. Fitzgerald made another note.

"And what do you know about Ethan Gray's activities that night?" Stanton asked. Zoe shifted on the staircase, and the wood creaked. Cara willed herself to look Stanton in the face. Why were they asking about Ethan? Suddenly an image flashed into her mind of Ethan, crouched on the bench in the training room this morning. *I feel so guilty,* he'd sobbed. No. No, that was impossible.

"I don't know what you mean," she almost whispered.

"Honey! Did you talk to Ethan at the party?" Mom chimed in anxiously.

Cara nodded. "Yes, I talked to him. We stood in the kitchen and talked for a while." She thought of the black square of the window over the sink. The backyard, gray in the twilight. The black hair, the same hair she'd known all her life, disappearing behind the garage. "He said he'd walk me home." *Ethan's never going to make a move on you as long as his nasty girlfriend is around.*

"And did he?" Stanton asked. Fitzgerald was scribbling furiously on his pad.

"Did he what?"

Stanton gave her a look. "Walk you home."

Cara nodded. "Yes, he did."

"And what time was that?" Stanton asked.

"Um, I'm not totally sure. Around eleven." Cara couldn't believe how calm her voice sounded.

Fitzgerald looked up from his notes. "And how did Alexis seem at the party, Ms. Lange?"

Everyone looked at Cara. The moment spun out in endless ticks of the mantel clock. "Like her regular self." It wasn't really a lie. Alexis was *always* a bitch. As she justified the omission of their fight, Cara's eye twitching slowed, then stopped.

Fitzgerald snapped his notebook closed and nodded at Stanton. They both stood up. Fitzgerald tucked his pen into his breast pocket. "Thank you, Ms. Lange."

Mom showed them to the door. "If there's anything more we can help you with . . ." Her words trailed off.

The officers nodded. "We'll be in touch," Stanton said. The door swung closed behind them.

Cara and her parents stood in the front hall like actors

waiting for their next cue. "Well!" Dad said finally. "This is terrible. I'm glad you could help them, Cara."

She nodded. The pressure in her chest felt like it was going to crush her. "I really have to go to the bathroom," she blurted. Turning, she ran up the stairs, ignoring their astonished stares below.

Cara burst into her room. "Where were you on Saturday night?" she barked.

"Don't shout. They'll hear you," Zoe replied calmly. She turned from the window, where she was gazing out at Sydney's house. "The guy cop was kind of cute, didn't you think?"

"Zoe, be serious!" Cara went up to her friend and looked right into Zoe's violet eyes. The whites were bloodshot. "I need to know. Where did you go on Saturday night?" She grasped Zoe's arm.

Zoe jerked her arm away. "Get off me. I already told you. I hung out at the barn for a while, and then I came back here."

"Where did you get that pearl?" Cara shot back.

"I *told* you. From my mom." Zoe's eyes narrowed. "Why are you giving *me* the third degree?" She paused. "It's Ethan you really should be worried about."

Cara backed away. "What do you mean? That Ethan actually could have . . ."—she couldn't say "killed"—"done something to Alexis?"

I did something bad, Cara. But it's not anything worse than what he did to me.

Zoe shrugged and picked up an eyeliner lying on Cara's dresser. She gazed in the mirror above Cara's vanity and drew a heavy black line above her eye. Her raccoonlike eyes seemed to take up half her face. "Well, that's kind of what the police were saying, right?" She put the eyeliner down and gazed at her friend. "I'm just trying to help you out here, Car. How about a little loyalty for your best friend?" She studied Cara and smiled suddenly. "Want to do cucumber masks?" She held up a half-squeezed tube. "I found this in your drawer this morning."

Cara nodded dumbly. She allowed herself to be led over to a chair and closed her eyes as Zoe laid a hot, damp washcloth over her face. It smelled mildewy. Under the thick covering, she felt Zoe pressing her hands over her face. It felt like being buried alive.

Chapter 18

CARA THRASHED IN THE TWISTED COVERS THAT NIGHT, unable to banish the images of Ethan, handcuffed, being shoved into a cell. Or standing in front of a tall courtroom bench, hands shackled to a chain around his waist, wearing an orange prison jumpsuit, head bowed as the judge read out his sentence. She pushed the blankets off, lying splayed out in her T-shirt. Ethan couldn't have done something to Alexis, could he? He was the gentlest guy she'd ever met. *But even gentle people can sometimes snap,* her mind argued. That's what Zoe would say. And he'd admitted to having a bad temper. . . .

Cara shivered suddenly as a draft cooled the sweat on her body, and she pulled up the covers over her clammy skin. All the while, Zoe slept peacefully beside her, hair striped over her face, hands tucked under her cheek as if she was posing for a Hallmark card. Finally, as gray and pink began to lighten the eastern sky, Cara crept from between the covers and stole downstairs to the silent kitchen.

Samson was crouched on the kitchen counter, his yellow

eyes alert, squatting on what Cara first thought was a nest of shredded blue paper. Then she realized it was her gym bag. It was ripped to shreds, ruined, and covered with gray cat hair.

Rage welled up inside her. Her favorite bag, the one she used every day, and this hideous animal dared to just stare up at her placidly like he'd done nothing wrong. "Damn you!" she yelled. She swatted at him, and he hissed and batted her hand away with his paw. She shoved him off the counter as hard as she could. He splatted to the floor, scrambling on the linoleum with his back paws, and fled into the living room.

Cara's face was so hot she could hardly see. She grabbed the shredded bag from the counter and shoved it into the garbage can under the sink. She slammed the cabinet door so hard it bounced open again. Clenching her fists, Cara stood a moment, fighting to keep from dumping the entire garbage can out onto the floor. After a minute, her pulse slowed to a safer rate, and she carefully closed the cabinet door again and found the Cheerios in the pantry.

She poured some into a bowl and hunched at the kitchen island, blankly spooning the cereal into her mouth. She stared down at the little brown o's floating in the puddle of milk at the bottom of her bowl and rubbed her temples with her fingers. In just two hours, she would walk into English class. Ethan would either be there . . . or he wouldn't.

Mom came into the room, wearing jeans and a sweater, her face still lined with sleep. She went straight to the sink and began filling the coffee maker. "Cara, I just got off the phone with Kathy Henning. They've organized a search party for today. It sounds like the whole community is involved. Anyway, your father and I are going to join it. I think it would be nice if you did also. You can miss school this one day." She thrust the coffeepot onto the burner and pressed on.

"Okay," Cara said. An image flashed into her mind of herself, searching the creek bed. Stumbling onto Alexis's white hand, sticking out from under a log, the water flowing over it. The Cheerios churned in her stomach. She swallowed hard.

"Everyone is meeting at the Methodist church at nine," Mom continued, opening a bag of bread. "Dad and I are going over early to help Kathy organize."

After Mom and Dad left, calling out that they would see her in an hour, Cara continued sitting alone at the kitchen table. Something kept her from going upstairs to her room. She didn't want to be with Zoe right now, didn't want to sit on the edge of the bed watching her breathe, as she knew she would do if she went upstairs. Through the open window, she could hear people walking by outside, talking. Cars drove up the street, more frequently than usual. Everyone was getting ready for the search.

Cara sat still as the furnace clicked on and then off, and the kitchen clock counted off the seconds, then the minutes. Two minutes passed, then another. When the clock read 8:45, she slid off her stool, grabbed her phone from the front table, and laced up her sneakers. She pulled Dad's barn jacket from the front closet and left, shutting the door against the heavy silence in the house.

Outside, it was a crystal autumn day. The sky soared overhead with that deep, soul-stirring blue you only see in the fall. Mums and asters waved from the flowerbeds, and the lawns were still bright green. Leaves were piled high in big, crackly piles at the curbs. Here and there, a pile was squashed where a kid had jumped in it, the leaves spilling out onto the street.

Even from a block away, Cara could see that the Methodist parking lot was full of cars. The front lawn of the church looked like a carnival waiting to happen. Everyone wore jackets and ball caps and stood in somber little groups, talking with their hands in their pockets. German shepherds strained on leashes, and around the corner, Cara saw a half dozen horses pulled up in a circle, their riders chatting quietly as their mounts slung their heads and pricked their ears at the unfamiliar noises and smells.

A big folding table had been set up near the front steps of the church. The Hennings stood behind it, greeting people as they arrived. There was something that looked like a sign-in sheet, and a stack of fliers with a fuzzy black-and-white picture of Alexis. Her own parents were off to the side. Mom was manning a big carafe of coffee, pouring it into paper cups, while Dad rummaged through a cardboard box filled with sugar packets, stir sticks, and creamer.

Sarit and Madeline were standing under a tree at the edge of the lawn with a bunch of other Sherman students. Sarit waved, and Cara nodded, but she didn't go over. There was only one person she wanted to talk to. She swept her eyes over the lawn again, but Ethan was nowhere in sight. She didn't dare think about where he might be.

Then a man Cara recognized as Alexis's uncle climbed the steps of the church, a paper in his hand. "Attention, everyone!" He waved his arms, and the crowd grew quiet. "Thank you, everyone, for coming. This is a terrible time for our family, and it is only the support of our community that is enabling us to get through it. The searchers will be broken into four groups, and those groups will cover Shelton Woods, French Park, the riverbank, and Mill Creek. Thank you to those who brought horses. If you could please take the steep hillsides, that would be wonderful." The man continued reading from his paper, running through instructions.

The lawn started emptying out. The dog people divided themselves up between the groups, while the horses went off toward the hilly areas of the woods. Cara still hadn't put her name on the list—she just didn't want to get that close to Mr. and Mrs. Henning—but as the searchers divided themselves into the four groups, she tagged along on the edge of the group searching the park.

Once they reached the big open space, the leader, a young mom with a baby in a backpack, instructed everyone to form a long line stretching across the park. They were to walk slowly, with their heads down, examining the ground as they walked. If anyone found anything suspicious, they were to call out so that the leader could mark the spot for the police.

Cara took an end position at the edge of the park, next to a skinny, gray-haired man wearing battered motorcycle boots. The woods were to her left. She could hear the searchers from that area snapping branches and calling to one another. She felt a fleeting thankfulness that the search area wasn't near the old barn. What if Zoe decided to take another unscheduled excursion today?

At the signal from the leader, the group began walking. Cara walked slowly, examining the soggy grass, her sneakers squishing into it step by step. Next to her, the motorcycle boots kept pace. Beyond those, a pair of tasseled loafers were getting soaked as their owner walked.

Then, a pair of trail-running sneakers appeared on Cara's other side. Cara stopped short and looked up, right into Ethan's blue eyes.

Her hand flew to her mouth. "Oh my God, it's you!" she almost screamed. The motorcycle-booted man shot her a startled look, and Ethan pulled Cara by the arm into the cover of the woods.

Cara resisted the urge to throw her arms around him and settled for mumbling, "I didn't see you earlier." He looked exhausted. His hair was matted, and his clothes were rumpled, as if he'd slept in them. He shivered a little in his thin jacket as a brisk wind blew, rattling the bare branches. Through the brambles separating them from the park, Cara could see the searchers marching past, calling to one another. One of the horses walked by, his bridle jingling and his hooves squishing in the boggy ground.

Cara hugged her arms across her chest. For a long moment, she searched his face for any clue about where he'd been. But his eyes were dull. They betrayed nothing.

"The police came to the house last night," she said finally.

He nodded. "Yeah. They went around to a bunch of houses—all of Alexis's friends."

"What—what happened?" Cara whispered. He looked so beaten down, like a dog who'd been kicked too many times and couldn't get back up again.

Ethan sat down on a log behind him and rested his forearms on his knees, staring down at the forest floor. Gingerly, Cara perched next to him. The soggy moss coating the top of the log squished under her rear. She could feel the wetness seeping through her jeans. But she didn't care. The only thing that mattered was Ethan, here beside her.

He took a deep breath. "They came over about eight and told me I had to come down to the station for questioning. There were two of them. A woman, Stanton, and—"

"Fitzgerald," Cara supplied.

Ethan nodded. "Right. My parents were freaking out, but the cops kept saying I wasn't being arrested, that they just wanted to ask me some questions. They might as well have arrested me though, because that's sure as hell how they were acting. . . ." His voice trailed off, and after a moment's hesitation, Cara put her hand on top of his. The skin was dry and smooth. He squeezed her hand back, almost convulsively, clutching at it as if it were a lifeline. The words tumbled from his mouth. "They put me in this little room, just like in the movies, and kept asking me over and over what happened that night. It was like they were expecting me to say something different, but all I could tell them was the truth."

She held her breath. "What—what was the truth?" Her voice shook a little. She couldn't bear it, just couldn't, if Ethan had done . . . *something* . . . to Alexis.

His brow creased. "You know. Alexis and I had that fight, and then I walked you home. And then I went home and fell asleep." Ethan shook his head. "I felt like a criminal. Like I was covering something up even though there was nothing to cover up. I felt like they were going to catch me."

"It sounds so awful." Cara squeezed his hand.

He nodded. "It was. But it could have been so much worse, if it wasn't for you."

"Me?"

"You told them I walked you home—it's my alibi. Without

155

that, I don't even know what could have happened." Spontaneously, he leaned over and kissed Cara's hand. His lips were soft and she felt the brush of his hair on her wrist.

Ethan looked up at her, his blue eyes anxious. "Cara, *you* don't think I did anything to Alexis, do you?" His grip on her hand tightened.

Cara stared right into his blue eyes. She could see all the way to the bottom. She shook her head. "Ethan, I know you didn't."

He reached out and hugged her. "Thank you. Thank you." For a long moment, they remained still, his face buried in the crook of her neck. She felt his hot breath on her skin. Then he lifted his head. His face was streaked with tears.

Cara stared at him. The Ethan of her dreams had disappeared. He was just another person who was sad. She was kind of glad, actually. Dreams disappeared when you woke up. The real thing was better anyway.

Cara reached out and wiped away one of the tears with her sleeve. He smiled. "You must think I'm a real mess," he said, sniffling once.

She shook her head violently. "No, I'd never think that. You've had an awful night." Cara looked out through the branches at the park where the search was continuing. "And unfortunately, it's not over."

Ethan followed her gaze. The bright jackets of the searchers were visible as dots of color on the autumn landscape. In the distance, one of the German shepherds barked. Ethan sighed. "Hey, did you hear anything more about the Sydney investigation?" His voice sounded normal again.

Cara shook her head. "Nothing. I guess they're still working on it."

"I kept expecting the cops to ask me about that, too, but they never mentioned it." Ethan stood up and held out his hand. "You think we should get back?"

Cara nodded and allowed him to pull her up. Slowly, they pushed their way out of the woods and began trudging through the wet grass again, heads down, searching for a scrap, a clue, anything that would tell them where Alexis was.

Chapter 19

AFTER FOUR HOURS, CARA'S JEANS WERE SPLASHED UP TO her knees. Her shoes were soaked through to her socks, and she had a big scratch across her cheek where a blackberry bramble had whipped her in the face. And there was no sign of Alexis. There'd been some excitement when one of the dogs had stumbled on a bone, but it turned out to belong to a deer carcass lying a few feet away. By three o'clock, the search began to break up. People straggled home across the park, and back at the Methodist parking lot, cars pulled out one by one until only the Hennings and Cara's parents were left, wrapping the coffee carafe and collecting the torn and damp fliers from the lawn. Ethan had to go after getting a call from his mom.

Mom and Dad promised to go to dinner with the Hennings. With relief, Cara walked home slowly. The foyer was deserted, with only a round dent on Samson's usual bed on the hall chair. She went straight to her room. She ached all over, her feet were freezing, and all she wanted was a hot bath and her robe. Then some dinner and the sofa with the TV on, getting lost in some stupid romantic comedy where people didn't show up dead in pools or go missing in the middle of the night.

But her room was deserted—again. "Damn it!" Cara slammed her backpack to the floor. It was so stupid and dangerous for Zoe to be running around, especially today when all of those people were out. Especially if she really did do something bad back at home. Cara had done her best not to pry into Zoe's past. But if Zoe really had committed some kind of crime, it was going to catch up to her eventually. The police were everywhere. She couldn't stay hidden forever. And apparently, she didn't want to.

The anger built in Cara's head until she turned and ran out of the room in a white heat. She pounded down the stairs and back out the front door, her wet sneakers slapping the floor.

Outside, the sky had grown overcast, the brilliant colors of the morning replaced by muted shadows. The sun was low in the sky. Cara ran down the street, past the school and the water tower and down the steep slope to the farm fields. There was nothing charming about the scene today—just dead, brown goldenrod and crashed-over clumps of yellow grass. She ran through the fields, her breath whistling in her throat.

The barn was visible ahead. Cara pulled up as she reached it. She wasn't surprised to find the door partly open. "Zoe?" she called. Turning sideways, she squeezed in through the crack. Damn, it was dark in here. "Zoe?" she called again. There was no answer, just a rustling. Cara's heart started beating faster, and suddenly she didn't want to be alone in the dark anymore. Bracing her back and her feet, she shoved open the heavy sliding door until gray light flooded the space.

Zoe stood in the middle of the straw-strewn floor, wearing

one of Cara's lace camisoles and flip-flops in spite of the cold. She had Samson in her arms.

"What are you doing?" Cara demanded. "Do you realize how dangerous it is for you to go out today? What's the deal, Zoe? Do you actually want to be caught?" She paced the floor, her anger snapping from her like sparks.

"I'm sorry," Zoe said in a little-girl voice. She pushed out her bottom lip and squeezed the cat in her arms. Samson struggled. "No, no, little kitty. Stay with Auntie Zoe." She turned him upside down and cradled him like a baby. Samson flattened his ears and swiped at her with his claws extended.

"What are you doing here?" Cara demanded.

Zoe shrugged. "Just hanging." Samson yowled and raked her forearm with his claws. Zoe dropped him abruptly on the ground. "Stupid cat." He fell awkwardly and ran out of the barn, his tail swollen like a big brush.

Zoe came up to Cara. Her hair was greasy, and her camisole was stained with food. She'd put her hair up in an elaborate bun on top of her head, with messy strands hanging down all around her face. Cara could see the dandruff and grease in it. Her mascara was smudged in big rings around her eyes, which made her violet eyes look huge. Cara wrinkled her nose as Zoe came closer. She smelled like underarms and unwashed laundry, all overlaid with the powerful scent of Shalimar. Someone had given Cara a bottle one Christmas, and she'd never touched it. Zoe must have found it in her dresser.

Zoe came closer. A wave of light-headedness passed over Cara, and for a moment she swayed on her feet. "I've missed you," Zoe crooned. She reached out and caressed a lock of Cara's hair. Her fingernails were broken, one almost to the

161

quick, but she hadn't bothered to bandage it. "I was so lonely without you today." She stepped closer. Cara could feel her hot breath on her cheek.

A wave of nausea enveloped her, and she pulled away. Quickly, she turned her back on Zoe and walked over to one of the glassless windows. She leaned out and breathed deeply of the cold, clean air that smelled only of wet earth and leaves.

When her stomach was no longer threatening to reverse itself, Cara turned back to Zoe. She was squatting on the floor now, picking at one of her toenails.

"Zoe, what's the deal? Do you have a plan? How long do you think you'll be staying here?" The words came out sharper than Cara intended, and she watched in dismay as Zoe's face crumpled. Her eyes filled.

"What's the deal with *you*, Cara?" she sniveled. Muddy tears rolled down her face and into the front of her shirt. "I thought we were best friends, and now you're kicking me out?"

"No, wait. That's not what I meant. I just meant . . . I don't know." She paced to the other end of the barn.

"We're best friends, Cara, aren't we?" Zoe's voice behind her was thick with tears. Cara turned around. Zoe was still squatting on the ground, her arms around her knees. A bubble of green snot formed over one nostril. Cara grimaced.

"Look, Zoe, I'm just saying this because you seem . . . not happy," Cara tried. "It seems like it's stressful for you, being here. Maybe if we thought about it, we could figure out somewhere else for you to go."

Zoe swiped the back of her hand under her nose. "There's nowhere else for me to go," she said. She sounded tired all of a sudden. "But I'll go if you want me to. I guess you do want me

162

to, now that you've got other friends and a boyfriend. You're right—you must be sick of me." She got to her feet. Her camisole shifted, hanging down to reveal her bony chest. A deep scar Cara didn't remember ran down her sternum. Cara winced and looked away.

"I just need to get my stuff out of your room. Then you won't have to see me again." Zoe turned toward the door.

"Zoe, wait." The words came out of Cara's mouth as if someone else were speaking. "Don't."

Zoe stopped but didn't turn around. Cara put her hand on her friend's shoulder. Her skin was cold and damp, like a frog's.

"I'm sorry," Cara said softly. "I'm sorry, Zo." She sighed. "It's just . . . it's been a long day, okay? I'm really stressed out over the whole Alexis situation."

Zoe turned around. Her tears were gone. "Did you see Ethan at the search party?" she asked brightly.

Cara blinked at the sudden shift. "Um, yeah, I did," she said slowly. "He had a really rough night. The police—"

"Uh-huh, uh-huh." Zoe nodded her head rapidly. "I see. Really stressed about Alexis, huh, Cara? Or is it Ethan? You should be happy, you know. You have everything you want now that Alexis is gone. Or do you wish I hadn't—" She stopped.

Cara stared at Zoe. Her friend's eyes were dry now, her smile was wide. She looked around the barn. "I wonder where Samson went. Kitty!" Her voice echoed in the rafters. She looked at Cara. "I can't leave without him. Will you help me look, Cara? Then we can go back to your room. And you can tell me what you and Ethan talked about."

Cara nodded. That's what Zoe wanted. So that's what she was going to do.

Chapter 20

"I HEARD SHE WAS, LIKE, SLEEPING WITH GUYS FOR drugs and one of them kidnapped her."

"Really? Tara said that she had a secret boyfriend in San Francisco. She stole her parents' car and ran away to be with him."

Cara closed her locker door slowly as she caught a shred of the latest rumors on Alexis's disappearance. It had been like this nonstop since the search party on Tuesday. Now it was Thursday, and still all anyone could talk about was Alexis, Alexis, Alexis. The school was covered in green ribbons, Alexis's favorite color, symbolizing their hope for her safe return. The teachers had them pinned to their clothes. The missing person posters were tacked to every bulletin board. Cara felt Alexis's eyes watching her as she passed through the halls. Even in the cafeteria, the mood was subdued. For the most part, people ate and left. It was like the whole school was holding its breath until Alexis was found.

Cara realized she'd closed her locker without taking out any of the books she needed. She opened it again. She'd been doing that sort of thing a lot these days, like she was walking around half-asleep.

She pushed open the school's heavy front door and stopped short on the steps. Her mouth went dry. In front of her stretched a long street, a mile or two straight, and it was thickly lined with telephone poles. On every pole, a missing-person poster of Alexis was stapled. She was going to have to walk home through that tunnel of flapping posters, reaching out toward her, brushing her face like tentacles.

Cara blinked and shook her head. The nightmare scene evaporated, and the ordinary, tree-lined streets appeared in front of her. Just houses and lawns, like usual. God, she had to get some more sleep. She was daydreaming right here on the steps.

The way home was only three blocks, past the neat, quiet houses dozing with their shades half-pulled. The shouts of kids playing filtered from a backyard, but otherwise every door was shut. The sidewalks were deserted too. She rounded the corner. Her house loomed at the end of the block, like a fortress containing a mad princess. Zoe was in there.

Cara was almost home when she saw them. A dozen or so of the Alexis posters, stapled up on the trees all around her house. Mom must have done it. Now Cara really did have to walk through them to get to the house.

She could feel her heart start to pound. Sweat beaded the edge of her hairline. She felt a crazy urge to offer Alexis's photo a polite smile, as if she were meeting someone at a party she didn't really want to talk to. *It wasn't me, Alexis. It wasn't my fault.* Wasn't it? She willed her feet to keep walking and forced them past the last poster and up the porch steps. She sagged against the railing with relief.

166

Cara exhaled deeply as she opened the front door and closed it behind her. The silence of the house wrapped her like an embrace. She dropped her bag with a thud to the foyer floor and wandered into the kitchen, trying not to think about Zoe upstairs. She did that a lot these days—tried not to think about Zoe. She didn't know what else to do.

Cara extracted a can of Diet Coke from the fridge and popped it open, taking a long gulp. She stuffed a handful of saltines in her mouth and idly snapped on the TV over the microwave. Oprah interviewing Kofi Annan, a perky TV chef showing how to make a castle out of Jell-O, a sobbing woman talking directly to the camera. Cara's fingers froze on the remote. She willed herself not to click back to the sobbing woman. Her fingers didn't listen. She clicked back.

"And please, please, if anyone has any information, any at all, if they could call this number," Mrs. Henning choked out. "My daughter could be anywhere, hurt, and alone . . ." Her voice trailed off, consumed by weeping. Cara stood frozen in front of the TV, the remote slack in her fingers. Alexis's mother looked terrible—her hair was a mess, and her eyes were puffy, red slits. Beside her, Mr. Henning patted her shoulder as he stared at the ground. He had aged a decade since Sydney's memorial last week. His silver-haired, tanned elegance was gone. He looked like a beaten-down old man.

With trembling fingers, Cara carefully replaced the remote on the counter. She didn't feel like a snack anymore. She left the saltines on the counter and climbed the stairs to her room. She didn't want to go up there. She didn't want to see Zoe. But she had to. She had to talk to her.

Slowly, Cara opened the door to her room. Flickering red

light came pouring out, and for one confused moment, she thought the room was on fire. She pushed opened the door the rest of the way and saw that Zoe had lit candles everywhere. The shades were drawn, and the lights were out.

The fetid air assaulted Cara in a wave as she stepped into the room. It smelled of stale breath and old food and unwashed laundry. Every inch of the floor was littered with Cara's clothes. Her closet door hung open at a crazy angle—it had been partially pulled off its hinges. The empty hangers twisted on the clothes rod. The dresser top and desk were covered with food-caked dishes. Glasses cloudy with fingerprints cluttered the bedside table. When had it gotten this bad? Had it always been like this? Cara couldn't remember. She felt dizzy, disoriented.

Zoe was squatting on the floor, a paper spread in front of her. She looked up as Cara came in, her eyes glassy bright. "Hi." She smiled. "I've been waiting for you." She was wearing Cara's mother's black silk bathrobe.

Cara focused on the bathrobe. "Where did you get that?"

Zoe shrugged. "From your mom's closet."

"Zoe, you can't just go snooping around during the day when no one's here," Cara started to say. Then she saw what Zoe had in front of her. It was the missing person poster, and Zoe was coloring it in with markers. Cara watched, frozen, as Zoe carefully traced Alexis's eyes with blue, humming a little tune in her throat.

Zoe looked up and saw Cara staring at her. She smiled sweetly. "I always thought she'd be prettier with blue eyes."

Bile filled Cara's mouth and she swallowed hard, shuddering at the taste. "What the hell are you doing?" She leaned

168

over and ripped the poster from Zoe's hands. "Don't you have any respect?"

Zoe didn't protest. She just watched, her eyes following Cara's every move. Cara stared at the poster in her hands. It was the first time she'd examined one this closely. Alexis was standing outside somewhere, wearing a plaid shirt. Her face was caught in a half-smile, and her hair was blown back from her face in the wind. Her eyes looked huge and dark, haunted. *What have you done, Cara?* she seemed to be asking.

Cara shook her head so violently her teeth clacked together. Nothing. She hadn't done anything! *But you know who did, Cara.*

"No!" Cara shouted aloud. Heat filled her body, and without thinking, she ripped the paper into shreds, scattering them over the bed. From her perch, Zoe watched attentively, her head to one side, alert as a little bird.

Cara stared down at the scraps, her chest rising and falling. Alexis's face was reduced to meaningless black marks on the twisted pieces of white paper. But from one scrap, her eye shone out. Cara stared at it, and Alexis's eye stared back at her. *Your fault, Cara,* the eye said.

"Stop it!" Cara screamed. She grabbed double handfuls of the paper scraps and ran into the bathroom, dumping them into the sink. Hands shaking, breath whistling in and out of her throat in half-sobs, she scrabbled frantically in the bathroom drawers. Finally, she found it—an old lighter. She flicked the stiff wheel once, twice—nothing. "Come on," she half-sobbed. Again—it lit. Cara lowered her hand into the sink and touched the scraps with the flame. She stood with her hands gripping the counter, the warmth of the fire bathing her face, the pounding of her heart finally slowing. The flames petered out. All that was left of Alexis was a heap of gray ashes.

Cara lifted her head just as a knock came at the door. She whirled around, her heart seizing up again. The knock came again. "Cara?"

It was Mom. Her voice was insistent, and worried.

"Cara!"

Before Cara could say anything, she heard the door open. She squeezed her eyes shut and waited for Mom's scream as she saw Zoe. But there was no scream. Just silence. Cara opened her eyes and cautiously peered around the bathroom door.

Mom was standing there, still in her gray suit, her briefcase dangling from one hand. The back of the other hand was pressed against her mouth. She turned to look at her daughter, and Cara started. Mom looked as if she was about to cry.

"Cara," she half-whispered. "Your room . . ."

Cara darted a quick glance around. Zoe was nowhere to be seen. She must be under the bed. Mom's gaze took in the destroyed closet, the dirty dishes, the bed with its unwashed sheets.

Carefully, Mom set her briefcase by the door and stepped over the heaped clothes on the rug. She perched at the edge of the bed. It was odd seeing her sitting there, instead of Zoe. "Honey, tell me what's wrong," Mom said. Her mouth was taut. She knotted her hands together in her lap, as if bracing herself, her eyes searching Cara's face.

Cara swallowed. She could almost see Zoe's eyes glowing from under the dust ruffle. But when she blinked, the eyes were gone.

"Cara!" Mom's voice was sharp.

Cara jumped. "Huh?"

"Your room, honey, we're talking about your room." Mom's voice cracked. She controlled herself with a visible effort. "Focus, okay? What's been going on in here?" She swept her hand around.

Cara took a deep breath. When she spoke, she was surprised to hear her voice coming out calm and strong. "I know it's a little messy, Mom. Sorry about that. I've just been really busy with track and school, and I haven't had much time to clean. I'll take care of it, I promise."

Mom shook her head. "I just want to know that you're okay. This doesn't look like okay to me."

"I'm fine!" The eyes under the dust ruffle were back. Cara controlled her voice. "I'm fine," she said, lower.

Her mother sighed and stood up. "I'll believe you're fine when I see you're fine. For now, I'm going to have to talk to your father." She picked up her briefcase. "I'm worried, Cara. I'm very worried." She opened the door, and Cara closed it with exquisite care behind her.

Chapter 21

ATTENDING CLASSES ON FRIDAY WAS A SHAM. SHE COULDN'T concentrate on anything. They were closing in on her. Mom would try to talk to her again today after school, she just knew it. Dad would get involved. After that, it was only a matter of time before they discovered Zoe.

It wasn't until track practice that Cara was able to think about something else. The sun shone on her hair, and the fresh autumn breeze made it possible for her to believe her world wasn't about to crumble around her.

"Come on, hup, hup!" Coach Sanders called. He clapped his huge, meaty hands, and Cara winced. Every sound seemed to pierce her eardrums. She stood grouped on the track with the rest of the girls. She'd forgotten her cozy warm-ups, and now she stood, cold and exposed, waiting for Coach to give them instructions.

"Four by four hundred relays, everyone," he ordered. "Count off." Cara was a three, along with Sarit and Julie. She didn't know when she'd felt less like running. And her eye was watering like crazy. Cara swiped at it and looked at her fingers. A crust of black mascara was smeared there. What the hell? She never wore makeup. Maybe it had come off of Zoe's face while she slept and gotten smeared onto Cara's. Or maybe Zoe was putting makeup on her while she slept. Anything seemed possible these days. Cara shivered and wiped her fingers on her shorts.

She had to do something about Zoe. Something was wrong with her. She couldn't deny it anymore. *Today,* Cara resolved. Today when she got home, she'd talk to Zoe about picking up the room. And she'd tell her . . . she'd have to leave soon. Cara's stomach curled at the thought of Zoe's reaction to this news. But she didn't have any choice. Zoe would have to leave as soon as she could find somewhere to go. It was for her own safety, anyway, now that Mom and Dad were closing in. No matter what she'd done back at her own home.

A loud blast on Coach's whistle right by her ear made Cara jump. She looked around. She was standing alone on the track. The rest of the team was already jogging to the other end to begin the relay drill. "Come on, Cara!" Coach pushed his face next to hers. "Move!"

Rage suddenly welled up in her, and she felt the overwhelming urge to leap on him, tearing his skin with her fingernails and biting . . . Cara shook herself. *Oh my God, you are really losing it.* She jogged after the team, not looking back for fear that the rage would return. Cara reached the other end of the track and took a deep breath, trying to calm herself. It was Zoe causing her so much stress. She just had to talk to Zoe.

The girls arranged themselves around the track for the relay. Cara stood near the bleachers. Julie was behind her and Sarit in front. She waited dully for the blast of Coach's whistle.

When it came, she watched Julie running toward her as if she were running in a dream. Julie got larger and larger, the shiny orange baton grasped in her hand. Cara stood, watching her, not really thinking about anything.

Julie approached. She was close enough now that Cara could see her sweaty bangs flattened on her forehead. She was making motions with her hands, shouting something, but Cara couldn't make out what she was saying. Her lips moved, a fact Cara observed with detached interest. Then all the sound rushed back into the world, as if someone had turned the volume up. "Go, Cara, go!" Julie was shouting.

With a start, Cara realized she was supposed to be running. She turned and poised herself toward Sarit on the track, running a few steps until she felt the baton *thwack* solidly into her palm. She could hear the other girls cheering for their teams. She forced her feet down the track, but Sarit looked impossibly far away. The baton felt like a stick of iron in her hand, pulling down her entire shoulder and back. She felt one foot catch behind the other and watched the gritty asphalt of the track rise up toward her slowly. *I'm falling,* she realized. But she didn't really care.

"*Ooomph.*" Cara caught herself with her palms, feeling a bolt of pain shoot through her knee. She remained that way for a long moment, hearing the pounding of feet running toward her, before a warm hand touched her back. Cara pushed herself to sit and look up into Sarit's concerned brown eyes.

"Are you okay?" Sarit asked. Cara nodded and, with horror, felt a few tears squeeze out of the corners of her eyes. Jesus, what was the matter with her? Crying over a scraped knee like she was eight?

"All right, all right." Coach pushed through the little knot that had gathered around Cara. "Let's go, Lange, you okay?" He looked down at her dispassionately. "Damn it." He saw her shredded knee. "Go fix that up in the locker room. First aid kit in my office." He turned back to the rest of the runners. "Let's do the relay again, folks!" he shouted.

Cara turned and trudged off the track, following the narrow concrete path back to the school. Her knee throbbed at every step. She could feel a trickle of blood make its way down her leg, staining the edge of her sock.

She had almost reached the gym door when she heard her name called. She turned around. Sarit was hurrying up the path toward her. "Hey," she said breathlessly. "I told Coach I was getting my period. He can't argue with that one. I thought you might want some company."

Cara nodded, surprised. Sarit opened the door for her, and her little gesture of kindness almost made Cara start crying all over again. God, she was a mess.

The locker room was deserted, littered with open gym bags spilling shirts and shoes onto the floor. Here and there, a deodorant stick lay uncapped on the floor. Sarit gazed down at Cara's knee. "Wow, it's really bleeding," she said. "Here, sit down. I'll get the kit."

Cara sank down on a bench and examined her knee, wincing. A good square inch of skin was torn away. She could see the bits of gravel ground into the raw, red flesh. Sarit came back into the room with the first aid kit. She knelt on the floor in front of Cara and opened it up. Cara hobbled over to the sinks and wet a few paper towels, gritting her teeth as she dabbed at the bloody wound. Sarit handed her a bottle of peroxide, and

Cara poured it over her knee, watching as it foamed white. She dabbed on some antibiotic ointment, then covered the whole thing with a stiff white bandage.

Cara exhaled and sank down on the bench, her back slumped. Sarit perched next to her and patted her back. They were silent. Then Sarit said, "Hey, listen, a few of the other girls are coming over tonight to hang out. Do you want to come?"

Cara looked at her in surprise. "Sure . . . ," she said slowly.

Sarit smiled. "Good. This is just a really hard time for all of us, with Sydney dead and Alexis missing. We have to support each other right now."

Cara nodded. "Yeah. You're right."

Sarit stood up. "Seven, okay? We'll get some pizza, just hang out."

"Right." Cara stood up too. Hanging out with the girls, relaxing, eating pizza sounded like absolute heaven. She couldn't wait. But, she realized, she still had the talk with Zoe looming over her . . . and who knew what Zoe would do?

Chapter 22

THE FIRST THING SHE SAW WHEN SHE OPENED THE door at home was Mom on the couch in the living room. She had a stack of legal briefs on her lap, but as soon as she saw Cara, she set them on the coffee table. Warily, Cara put her track bag down by the door. For a tense moment, they eyed each other. Mom's face was tight. She cleared her throat.

"I've spoken with your father, Cara," she started. "He's very upset. I am too." Her gaze was aimed somewhere over Cara's shoulder. "We've been worried about you for some time now, and the state of your room yesterday just confirmed our concerns." Mom's face looked tired, her makeup smudged under her eyes and her lipstick faded to a dull pink.

Cara licked her lips. The air in the room was stagnant, stifling. Why didn't someone open a window? "Mom, it's like I told you yesterday. I've been really busy lately. But I'm fine! Actually, I've never been happier." She tried a reassuring smile, but the beads of sweat were gathering at her hairline.

Mom shook her head. "Don't lie to me, Cara." Her voice

rose slightly. "You're not fine. Anyone who saw your room yesterday would see that." Her hands trembled, and she wiped them on the side of her skirt. Little gray hairs stuck up from her bun, catching the light when she turned her head. "Your father and I think it's time you started seeing Dr. Samuels again. I know we haven't gone to him in a long time, but he can help you get back on track."

Cara felt claustrophobia crushing her. When they'd first moved here, she and her parents had gone to see Dr. Samuels every week. But the visits had tapered off after a while.

Cara gasped for breath, but her lungs felt as if they were being squeezed sideways. "No," she managed, holding her hands out in front of her and backing away toward the staircase.

Mom rose and followed. "It's not an option. This is how you were acting when we first moved here. You need help." She advanced, and Cara backed away up the stairs, holding the banister. All of her worst fears were surrounding her. Mom was going to come into her room. She'd find Zoe and take her away. It would be Cara's fault. And for harboring Zoe they'd take *her* away. She'd never see Ethan again. She tripped on the landing and clutched at the banister. "Mom, wait," she tried, holding out one hand. "It's not that bad."

"Stop it!" Mom almost shrieked. She kept coming, backing Cara up the stairs. They were almost to the top. "You're in denial. Look at this! Look at this mess! You need help—" She flung open the door to Cara's room and stopped short, her words cut off as if someone had clapped a hand over her mouth.

Cara peered around the doorjamb. The floor was clear—perfectly clear, for the first time since Zoe had shown up. And Zoe herself was nowhere to be seen. She must have heard the shouting below and hidden quickly. The closet door, partly open, had been placed back on the hinges. Every piece of clothing hung up inside was placed as perfectly as if it had been in a boutique. Even the hangers were facing the same way, and the clothes themselves were organized by type, then length, then color. On the floor of the closet, Cara's shoes were lined up like soldiers at attention. The dishes and glasses were gone. Cara didn't want to think about Zoe going down to the kitchen when she was gone, but apparently she had. The bed was made. The room smelled of nothing but fresh air from the open window.

Mom turned away from the door. She looked like she'd been slapped.

"I told you I'd clean it up," Cara said. She couldn't think of anything else. She swallowed, waiting. Mom stared at her. Cara felt some of her equilibrium flowing back. She made herself move closer to her mother. "Really, Mom, you're making it a way bigger deal than it is." She patted her mother on the shoulder.

Mom twitched, as if feeling a spider on her arm. She fell back a step. "I . . . I . . . we'll have to talk later." She fled down the stairs. A moment later, Cara heard the door to her study close.

Cara sat down shakily on the edge of the bed. Her pounding pulse slowed. She closed her eyes and gazed for a while at the comforting darkness on the inside of her eyelids. When she opened them, Zoe was perched on the dresser across the room, smiling and swinging her legs. Where had she been hiding?

"Hi," she said cheerfully. There were lipstick smears on her teeth. Her hair was wet, as if she'd taken a shower, but she must not have used any shampoo. The soles of her feet were black with sticky dirt. She wore a T-shirt and jeans, but her fly was open and the collar of the T-shirt was stretched out, hanging down to reveal her dingy gray bra.

"Where were you?" Cara responded instead.

"Bathroom." Zoe smiled and nodded as if she'd made a fantastic joke. She looked around the room. "Thought your mom would like it if I cleaned up."

"Yeah," Cara answered slowly. "Things were getting a little tense there for a while." She noticed a large picture on the nightstand that hadn't been there before and picked it up. It was a snapshot of her and Zoe from elementary school. Cara was straddling her bike, Zoe hanging on behind her. They stood outside Zoe's house, the sun shining. Both of them were laughing hysterically. Cara set the picture down slowly, leaning it against the lamp. She looked over at Zoe.

Zoe was watching her. "What do you think of the picture?" she asked. "I found it when I was going through some of your old stuff." She smiled, a normal smile, and all of a sudden, Cara could see her friend again, underneath the mess and all of the weirdness from the last week.

A rush of warmth overwhelmed her, and on impulse, Cara put her arms around Zoe and hugged her. Then she recoiled automatically. Zoe's skin was damp and cool, even though the room was warm. There was a mushiness about her, as if her muscle tone was utterly gone. Cara had the disturbing sense that if she put her finger on Zoe's arm and pressed down, she'd hit bone.

Cara gathered her strength for the brave speech about Zoe leaving that she'd been rehearsing all afternoon. Then she looked at her friend, who seemed very small and vulnerable huddled there on the bed. She closed her mouth. "I'm going out tonight," she said instead. She tensed her muscles, expecting rage.

Zoe nodded instead. "Okay. Where are you going?"

"Sarit's. She's having some girls over." Cara watched Zoe carefully. But there was still no explosion. Zoe just nodded again.

"Cool. Want me to pick out something for you to wear?"

"Sure," Cara responded wonderingly. She watched as Zoe opened the closet door and paged through the clothes rapidly, pulling out a drapey, emerald-green T-shirt and a pair of dark jeans. She tossed them onto the bed, then added a slim pair of silver hoops.

Cara nodded, still in wonderment. "That's perfect," she said.

"I'm still good for something, aren't I?" Zoe smiled. Cara smiled back. Zoe arranged herself on the bed, and Cara stood and pulled her sweaty jersey over her head. But something about Zoe's attentive gaze made her feel like she was doing a striptease.

"I just need to jump in the shower," she said, not looking at Zoe. She gathered up her towel and went into the bathroom, closing the door behind her and locking it. She stared in the mirror as the water heated up in the shower.

Her own pale face stared back at her. Her eyes were ringed in black circles, and her hair hung in strings. The wound on her knee smarted under the bandage. No wonder her parents had been worried. She did look like a girl in need of help.

Cara felt better once she was in the shower, scrubbing herself with peppermint body wash. She tilted her face under the water and inhaled deeply, letting the hot, steamy air fill her lungs. It was good that Zoe hadn't freaked out about her going to Sarit's. Maybe she was finally realizing that it was okay if Cara had other friends.

Cara rotated her face back and forth, letting the spray tickle her skin. Maybe she'd been too critical of the whole Zoe situation. Zoe definitely had problems, but really, if she thought about it, things were actually better since Zoe had come back. Alexis and Sydney were . . . gone . . . and things with Ethan were going better than she ever could have hoped. She had friends now, too. And she had Zoe again, even if she did act strange at times.

Cara stayed under the shower so long, her fingers began to wrinkle. Finally, the hot water began to run out, and she shut it off. She wrapped the towel tightly under her arms and opened the door, letting the steam from the bathroom billow into the room. She was temporarily blind for a moment, but when the steam cleared, she saw that Zoe had laid her clothes on her bed, the shirt neatly arranged above the jeans. A pair of black ballet flats lay at the end of either jeans leg, and above the neck of the shirt, silver hoop earrings were arranged as if on a head. It was as though Cara had lain down on the bed and then just disappeared, leaving only the clothes and jewelry behind.

Zoe sat beside the clothes, her back straight and her hands clasped as they had been before.

"Thanks," Cara said slowly.

"Sure," Zoe said. Her voice was eager.

Cara looked around the room, but it seemed weird to go into the bathroom to dress. She plucked the shirt from the bed and awkwardly tried to pull it over her head while still clutching her towel. She could feel Zoe's gaze on her. She managed to tug on the jeans while keeping the towel around her waist. The towel fell away, and Cara turned to face the wall to fasten her pants.

She felt better once she had her clothes on. Zoe got up and extracted the flatiron from the heap on Cara's dresser. "Come here, let me straighten your hair," she said. The metal plates sent up a puff of steam as they heated. Zoe clacked the metal plates together.

Obediently, Cara sat down in front of the mirror. She watched her reflection and Zoe's as her friend bent over her hair, already drying in puffy frizzes. Zoe lifted a section of hair near Cara's ear and closed the iron on it. *Pfff.* A small burst of steam rose in the air.

For a few minutes, she lifted and ironed as they sat in companionable silence. Cara watched Zoe's intent face as she worked. In the dim light of the room, she looked pretty again as she concentrated, her dark hair luminous and her purple eyes focused and calm. She seemed so peaceful, Cara finally felt she could ask the question that had been haunting her for the last few days. She couldn't go on anymore without knowing.

"Zoe," Cara said. Immediately her heart started hammering. *It's okay,* she told herself. *It's just an innocent question.*

"Hmm?" Zoe said. She kept ironing.

"Zo, listen, I know this is weird, but I just feel like I have to ask—" Cara could hear her voice quaver.

"Just spit it out already," Zoe said, not looking up. "And no, I'm not a crack addict, if that's what you're wondering." She closed the plates around a piece of hair on the nape of Cara's neck.

Cara forced a little laugh. "Listen, Zoe. Did you have anything to do . . . with . . . Alexis going missing?"

Just then, she felt a searing pain on her neck. She screamed and jerked away violently, knocking over her chair. She clapped a hand on the back of her neck as if to protect it.

Zoe stood there, holding the burning flatiron. "I'm sorry," she said, but she didn't look that sorry. "I must have had it up too high."

Instead of answering, Cara grabbed a hand mirror from her dresser and held it up, moving it around until she could see the back of her neck. A bright red burn mark stared back at her, a perfect rectangle the same shape as the tip of the iron plate. "Christ, Zoe!" The skin burned, the pain searing and fresh, as if Zoe were still holding the iron to it.

"I'm sorry," Zoe said again, calmly. She went into the bathroom and came out with a washcloth. "Here." She started to apply the cold washcloth to Cara's neck. Cara clapped her hand on her neck and jerked away. Zoe stopped. For a long moment, she and Cara stared at each other in the mirror, their eyes locked together. Then Cara moved her hand and allowed Zoe to press the washcloth to her neck.

"How could you even ask me that about Alexis?" Zoe asked. Her voice was sorrowful. Cara closed her eyes as the

186

cool of the washcloth slowly stopped the burning feeling on her neck.

"I-I'm sorry," she murmured. All she could think about was the pain. "It was a stupid thing to ask." A worm of fear coiled itself in her stomach.

"Yes, it was," Zoe agreed. She refolded the washcloth and pressed it to Cara's neck again. "It was a stupid thing to ask."

Chapter 23

"H EY THERE!" SARIT OPENED THE DOOR RIGHT away after Cara rang the bell. She was wearing a hooded sweatshirt that read JINGLE BALL 2010 and a pair of flannel pajama pants printed with faded hearts. Moose slippers poked out from the pant-legs. Cara looked down at her Zoe-styled ensemble.

"I guess I'm a little over-dressed," she said sheepishly.

"No, don't be silly." Sarit pulled Cara inside and closed the door. It was warm in the house and smelled deliciously of pizza. Cara could hear the buzz of voices from the basement. "Come on, everyone's downstairs." Cara followed Sarit's ponytail as she tripped down the carpeted steps.

Five or six of the track girls were sitting on the floor or sprawled on the couches around a big, low coffee table. A flat-screen TV played on mute. On the table, a stack of pizza boxes sat unopened, along with two liters of soda and a bag of chips. With a touch of relief, Cara saw that while most of the girls were wearing sweats and leggings, Julie had on jeans, too, and a nice top.

"Hey, Cara," Madeline greeted her.

"Hi." Cara nodded at the group. She perched on the edge of a sofa next to Madeline, who was staring at her phone.

"Oh my God, look at this," she said, turning the screen to Cara. "St. James totally kicked Country Day's ass this morning."

Cara looked down at the screen showing the local track standings. "That's so crazy—their best sprinter has shingles. I totally didn't see that one coming," she told Madeline.

"Come on, let's eat." Sarit opened the pizza boxes, and immediately the melty cheese and pepperoni smell wafted through the room. Everyone started grabbing slices. Cara took a small one and tried to take a bite without dropping sauce on her shirt.

"Dude, what was Coach Sanders wearing today?" Julie called out to the group. She got up and wiggled her hips back and forth. "Could those shorts have gotten any smaller?"

Everyone giggled. "He loves showing off his ass," Madeline agreed with a wink.

Sarit shrieked, "Ew!" and started laughing so hard she collapsed on the floor with a beaded pillow over her head.

"His cheeks were hanging out the bottom," Cara tried. Everyone tittered. She grinned.

"Nasty!" Rachael said. She was riding the exercise bike in the corner, pedaling backward.

Cara sat back and ate the rest of her pizza, letting the conversation wash around her. She felt like she was inhabiting a different body—someone who was bold and confident and daring. *Someone like Zoe.* Her jaws stopped chewing. She saw Zoe in her mind's eye, not the Zoe of today, in her dirty clothes and greasy hair, but Zoe as she was the first night she came back. Her long shiny hair hanging down her back, her violet eyes shining. A confident smile and a joke—or a hug—always at the ready. That was the Zoe she loved. That was the Zoe she missed.

Sarit reached for the stack of books under the coffee table and pulled out last year's yearbook. She flipped it open, and Cara caught a glimpse of the heavily autographed title page and inside cover, unlike the barren expanse of her own at home. "Okay, we're going to go through all the guys in the class," she announced, "and say who's hot or nasty. Everyone has to vote."

Oh God. Cara's stomach made a little dive. Everyone probably already knew she'd never been out with a guy, or even kissed anyone before. She could only keep the normal girl charade up for so long.

"Dave Alcorn." Sarit's manicured finger slid to the first photo in the junior class, a moon-faced guy with a unibrow.

"Nasty." Consensus on that one.

Next, a big blond with a sweet smile. "Mike Balducci." Sarit looked around. "Madeline wants to hit that."

Madeline turned a little pink. "He's so nice. He gave me a pen in trig today."

Sarit rolled her eyes, smiling, before she went on. She called out a bunch of other names—most were deemed nasty, though a few others made the cut. From her seat on the couch, Cara watched with something like excitement and something like dread as Sarit's Vamp-polished fingernail approached *him*.

"Ethan Gray." Sarit's finger stopped.

"Hot." Everyone agreed on that. Sarit looked around. "Caarraa." She drew the word out. "You're all over that, right?" She grinned.

"Yeah," Rachael chimed in. "I've seen you two talking."

Cara lowered her head. "I feel so guilty," she mumbled. "I mean, his girlfriend's missing. But I can't help it. He's, like, the nicest guy I've ever met."

"And the nicest guy you've ever gotten the Heimlich from!" Julie called out. Her volume control was permanently broken. She laughed, then seeing Cara just stare, the huge brocade pillow on her lap, she quieted down. "I'm sorry," she said. "I'm just kidding. If you want to know my opinion, Alexis was horrible. You deserve him."

Sarit gasped a little, but Madeline nodded. "Totally. Julie's right, Cara. I don't care that Alexis's missing. Why should a bitch like her get him? She treated him like crap anyway."

"Yeah, she did!" The words fell from Cara's mouth as if someone else were talking. Before she knew what she was doing, she threw the giant pillow across the room, where it bounced off the flat-screen. "Fuck off, Alexis!" she yelled. For one instant, everyone sat in stunned silence. And then the entire room broke out in cheers. Sarit launched herself over and hugged Cara with such force, they both fell onto the thick beige carpet. Everyone was clapping and patting Cara on the shoulders. She sat up, panting, a huge grin splitting her face. It was like redemption for all the humiliation Alexis had poured on her over the years.

The laughter trailed off into the occasional snort and giggle, while Cara lay on the floor, staring up at the underside of the glass coffee table. From this angle, it looked like it was ten stories up.

Then Julie's round face leaned over the edge of the couch. Her hair dangled over her shoulders, almost brushing Cara's chest. "Okay. Here's the real question: Have you kissed him yet?"

Everyone sat up attentively and looked toward Cara.

She felt her breath come faster just at the *thought* of kissing Ethan. "No. He likes my evil twin better."

Everyone laughed. Cara shrugged and tried to look nonchalant. As nonchalant as Zoe would.

"What are you waiting for?" Madeline said. "Just watch, Alexis's going to come back and steal him away again." Before Cara could react, Madeline reached across her lap and grabbed her bag.

"Hey," Cara said weakly.

Madeline held up Cara's phone. "Got it!"

Everyone else squealed and pounced. "Me! Me! I want to send it," Sarit shouted. She grabbed the phone from Madeline.

"Oh, wait," Cara tried, but she knew it was hopeless.

The girls crouched around Sarit, who peered at the tiny screen. "Do you have the team directory in here? Wait, don't answer, here it is. Okay, this is him." She tapped her cheek with her finger, then typed something and sent it. All of the girls screamed with laughter.

"Oh my God, what did you say?" Cara reached for her phone. This time, Sarit handed it over. Cara looked at the sent message.

Want to hang out tomorrow? It's Cara.

"Oh God." Cara dropped the phone. Just then, it buzzed

on the coffee table, skating around by itself like a large beetle. Everyone screamed like the house was on fire and grabbed for the phone at once. Sarit got to it first and pressed read. Cara hid her head in the pillow.

"'Sure. I'll pick you up tomorrow,'" she read in a loud, theatrical voice. Everyone started screaming and bouncing up and down like crazed monkeys. Cara screamed too.

"Oh my God, I have a date with Ethan Gray," she yelled. Julie grabbed her by the hands and started jumping up and down on the couch. Cara jumped too, until she fell into a recliner in the corner, exhausted, but exhilarated.

As she lay there, clutching her phone to her chest, she realized that not only did she have a date with Ethan tomorrow, but for a few brief minutes, she'd been a normal girl, just hanging out and laughing with her friends. Not a girl who was hiding a secret.

Not a girl who was hiding a fugitive.

Chapter 24

"CARA, ARE YOU SURE YOU'RE GOING TO BE ALL RIGHT?" Mom asked for the thousandth time the next afternoon. She looked over from the passenger seat as Cara leaned forward, trying to merge onto the busy, rush-hour expressway. There was a semi behind her, but she pushed the car forward anyway. She didn't want any delays getting her parents to the airport. She had to get back in time to get ready for her date with Ethan.

Mom was still talking nonstop. "You understand that I have to go, don't you, honey? It's the worst luck that this would happen just when Dad's gone too, but I just have to be there during Grandma's surgery tonight. Uncle Bruce can't make it up until tomorrow morning, but I'm going to leave as soon as he gets there. I'll be gone less than twenty-four hours, and Dad will be home from his conference Monday morning."

What benevolent god had arranged things so that Grandma Lynn slipped and broke her hip just at the exact right moment, Cara didn't know. But the timing could not have been better. Dad left this morning for a law conference in Phoenix, and Mom would be tending to Grandma. Her first date with Ethan, and no parents would be around to get in the way.

"Watch it, Cara!" Her mother gripped the door handle. Cara cut the Volvo in front of a silver minivan. The driver braked rapidly and blew his horn. Cara hung on to the wheel to keep the car from swerving into the next lane.

"Be careful!" Mom stared at her with her brows knitted.

Cara threw a quick glance at her mother and pressed the brake, slowing the car down as gently as she could. "Sorry," she said blithely. Mom was really starting to get on her nerves.

Her mother rustled around in her purse. "Let's go over this stuff once again," she said. Cara knew without looking that she was holding the all-important emergency number and instructions sheet.

"Mom, I've got it," Cara cut in. "You'll be at Grandma's, phone number on the sheet. Turn the heat down to sixty at night."

"No boys, no fires, no parties," her mother instructed. Cara smiled grimly to herself. It just showed how out of touch her mother was that she actually thought she needed to remind her about parties and boys. Like she'd ever had a party in her life. Boys, on the other hand . . . Cara smiled to herself. Well, maybe that warning wasn't so far off.

"Cara!" her mother shrieked, bracing her feet on the floor. Cara saw the taillights looming in front of her fast, much too fast, and hit the brakes, barely managing to stop before she smashed into the car in front of them.

"Sorry, sorry, Mom," she managed. She slowed to a crawl. The airport exit loomed ahead. With relief, Cara signaled and took the off-ramp.

"Cara, I'm worried about leaving you," Mom said. She twisted around to look her daughter in the face. Cara focused on the maze of terminal signs in front of her. The sky was leaden. A huge jet soared in overhead. From this angle, its engines looked as big as a house.

Mom went on. "I'm going to call tonight and first thing tomorrow. And, Cara, I want you to answer your cell every time. No messages, or I'm coming straight home."

"Okay, Mom," Cara said seriously, but a crazy urge to laugh bubbled to her lips. It was so kind of her mother to remove herself so promptly. She pulled up to the long line of cars idling in front of the terminal.

The unloading zone was crowded, with skycaps pushing huge carts of baggage, people busily hauling suitcases from trunks, little kids with backpacks running in and out of the automatic doors. Cara parked and opened the trunk. She got out and helped Mom haul her bag out of the car.

"Cara." Her mother cupped her daughter's face in two hands. "Honey, are you sure you're okay? You seem . . . not like yourself."

Cara looked away. The concern in her mother's cornflower-blue eyes was almost too much. For a moment, she wanted to rest her head on Mom's shoulder—something she hadn't done since fifth grade. But she shoved that thought away. Every moment was keeping her from her date with Ethan.

"I'm fine," she said brusquely. Her mother dropped her hands.

"I hope so," she said quietly, almost to herself. She picked up the handle of her rolling suitcase. "Cara, I love you."

"I know. Love you, too." Cara didn't think she could stand the strain another minute. Finally, *finally*, Mom rolled away through the wide glass doors. Cara stood at the curb, waving until she disappeared. The lessening of pressure was intense, as if someone had freed her from binding ropes. She jumped back into the Volvo and started the car.

Ethan was waiting.

Cara accelerated blindly toward home. Her mind was already buzzing: first a shower, then flatiron her hair, then clothes. She thought of the green jersey shirt she'd worn to Sarit's. That would be perfect. The traffic whooshed by, but her eyes were focused only on Ethan's image, dangling tantalizingly in front of her.

Then, suddenly, another image swam into her mind's eye. Zoe, sprawled on her bed, stroking Samson delicately. "You don't actually think you're going to leave me again, do you, Cara?" she purred. Cara slammed on the brakes. She'd driven right past her driveway.

Cara blinked and reversed, then pulled up in front of her house. As she turned off the car, the silence of the peaceful suburban neighborhood filled her head, stilling the frantic buzz of her thoughts. She couldn't believe she'd forgotten about Zoe. She felt a cold dread in the pit of her stomach, thinking of explaining that she was going out again.

Cara got out of the car and closed the door with a clunk that sounded loud in the quiet. She stood a moment in front of the house, her keys dangling from her fingers. All up and down the street, the mowed green lawns sat in neat squares in front of each individual house. No cars moved up and down the street. A mockingbird, perched on a telephone line, called once and then fell silent. Her own house sat patiently, as if waiting for something.

Cara opened the front door, and immediately the stench hit her fully in the face, as if she'd been smacked. She recoiled momentarily, and then moved forward, holding her sleeve over her nose. It was like stepping into a tomb. She glanced into the dark downstairs of the house. Everything was the same as when she'd left.

The stench increased as she climbed the stairs. Her own bedroom door was standing open, wide open. With a feeling halfway between dreaming and dread, Cara followed the smell past her room and into her parents' bedroom across the hall. She was not surprised to see Zoe seated in front of her mother's dressing table. Her back was to Cara. Cara's mother's red lace nightgown hung loosely on Zoe's skeletal frame, a gray fur stole draped around her neck.

Zoe wheeled around on the little stool at the sound of Cara's footsteps. Cara fell back a step, pressing her fist to her mouth to quell the scream that bubbled in her throat. Zoe's face was a horror mask of makeup. Lipstick was slashed almost from ear to ear, like a sick clown mouth. Eyeliner ringed her eyes and dripped down her face in black, streaky tears. Her hair stuck out from her head at jagged, crazy angles, and stuck in it were several large, glittering brooches. In front of her on the dressing table, Cara's mother's jewelry box stood open, the lid partially smashed. The tiny key that usually kept it locked lay on the floor at Zoe's feet, along with a hammer. Bracelets were stacked up Zoe's arms, and a dozen necklaces were draped around her neck like a breastplate. When she moved her head, giant chande-lier earrings clanked and swung.

Cara's eyes traveled down from Zoe's ruined face to the fur around her neck. Her mother didn't own any stoles. Suddenly, sickeningly, she realized what it was. *Samson*. His front feet and head hung down on one side, his back feet on the other. His neck hung at a crazy angle. His green eyes were already clouded and sunken back in his head.

Cara screamed as Zoe watched her, playing a little with Samson's ears, a bright, interested smile on her lips, as if she were hearing a rare bird call.

Abruptly, Cara stopped screaming. Her hand clutched her throat. Zoe waited.

"What did you do?" Cara gasped. Her throat hurt from screaming. She could hardly bear to look at Samson's head, dangling down on Zoe's chest, his whiskers just brushing the pale flesh of her upper arm. Cara shivered suddenly. Goose-bumps rose all over her body.

"Oh, this?" Zoe looked down at Samson. A smile cracked the lipstick smeared on her face. "He did rip up your bag, didn't he? You always hated him. *Meow!*" She leaped at Cara a little with a hiss, and Cara shrieked and cringed.

Zoe settled back on the stool. Laughing, she spun around again. "You know, most of this stuff is cheap crap." She pawed through the jewelry box. "I was hoping for some dia-monds." She picked up Mom's bottle of Chanel No. 5 and spritzed her neck delicately.

Cara backed away slowly. She kept her eyes fixed on the doorway. Her breath was coming in hitches. With one hand, she felt for the stair banister. Her feet twisted under her, and she stumbled backward on the stairs. She grabbed the banister and clung to it before she could fall.

Her breath whistling in her chest, Cara scrambled the rest of the way downstairs just as the doorbell rang. She ran toward it, almost clawing open the door. Ethan stood just outside, his broad chest looking very big and solid and safe. Cara hurtled herself at him, sobbing deep in her chest.

"Hey," Ethan said, startled. His hands came up around her. "Hey now," he murmured as he patted her back. "What's wrong?" He looked over her shoulder. Quickly, Cara reached behind her and pulled the door shut.

"Come on," she managed to say. "I've got to get out of here."

Chapter 25

ETHAN BLINKED BUT RECOVERED QUICKLY. "OKAY, yeah." He led her down the steps. "Where do you want to go?"

"Let's just walk, okay?" Cara started toward the sidewalk, trying to shake the image of Zoe's crazed face from her mind. She walked faster and faster down the quiet sidewalk until she felt Ethan's hand catch hers.

"Hey, slow down." He pulled her back until she was walking next to him. "Just relax." He put his arm around her shoulders and squeezed firmly. They walked in silence for several blocks. Cara was glad he wasn't pestering her with questions right away. She looked up at his strong face and his jaw, darkened with a few days of stubble. She felt the solid, reassuring weight of his arm around her shoulder, pressing into her collarbone. The horror of the bedroom scene receded a few notches in her mind, and she felt her body relax.

Ethan took her hand and pulled her across the street. "Where are we going?" Cara asked.

"Come on," he said. "Lamont Park is right here." He guided her toward the neatly groomed little park. In the summer, the place was alive with T-ball teams and kids scrambling over the jungle gym, their moms chatting on the benches. But today the playing fields were deserted. The jungle gym stood silently, the wood chips underneath smooth and undisturbed. The swings swung slightly in the breeze, silhouetted against the gray sky.

Cara sat down on one, grasping the cold chains. She dug her toe into the hollow that hundreds of little feet had made over the years. Ethan sat on the swing next to her. "So," he said, twisting first right, then left, "are you going to tell me what was wrong back there? You came out of the house looking like you were about to pass out." He looked down at her, his brows knit with concern.

Cara took a deep breath and shook her head. There was no way she could tell Ethan about Zoe. It would sound too crazy. "It's my . . . cat," she said slowly. "My cat just died." She could hear the sobs gathering in her voice. But they weren't for Samson, of course. "I found him right before you came." Her voice sounded silly and false to her ears. She looked down at the toes of her sneakers pushing into the dirt beneath her feet. "I know that sounds so stupid, being upset about a cat, when Alexis is . . . missing." She stumbled a little on the last word.

"No." Ethan shook his head emphatically. He twisted his swing to face her. "It's okay. Don't worry like that." He reached out and took her hand. She could feel his warm dry fingers close around her cold ones. She squeezed his hand tight.

"Do—do you think about Alexis?" she asked, almost in a whisper. The words seemed to flow out of her mouth unbidden. She waited for his answer, watching his face.

"Sometimes," he said, low. "Sometimes . . . I think about you." His face was close to hers now, so close she could almost feel the heat of his breath against her cheek. She waited, trembling as he stroked her thumb with his own. She imagined she could hear his skin rasping against hers. "Cara, I don't know how I would have gotten through this last week without you."

She stared at him. His face seemed huge, filling up her field of vision. He leaned over, and she closed her eyes. She felt his lips press down on hers. His mouth was cool and tasted like apples. Suddenly, she thought of kissing Zoe in the barn—her cold lips and fetid breath. Her breath caught suddenly, and she pushed the image away with all her strength.

Ethan must have sensed something. He drew back and looked down at her questioningly. She stared up at him, then stretched up toward him, lifting her face. Telling him she wanted more.

He was kissing her again. She felt his hand on the back of her neck, then in her hair, pulling her closer to him. She tilted her head and opened her lips slightly. His mouth pressed harder on hers.

They broke apart. Cara tried to control her breathing. Ethan was breathing hard too, his face dark and intense. He opened his mouth to say something, but before he could, a police siren wailed nearby. They both looked up to see a cruiser driving slowly down the street.

It pulled up at the curb in front of the park. The siren

stopped, but the lights kept going, flashing red, then yellow, then blue, over and over. Two cops got out of the car. Even from this distance, Cara recognized the figures of Stanton and Fitzgerald. Her mouth went dry. Her fingers tightened around Ethan's.

They watched the cops approach over the dry grass, their navy-clad figures sharp and defined against the soft autumn landscape. They stopped in front of the swings.

"Ethan, we've been looking for you." Stanton stepped forward. "We're going to have to ask you to come with us, Mr. Gray. Just down to the station for a few questions."

Ethan looked from one cop to the next. "Can I ask what this is about?"

The officers' expressions were blank. "I'm afraid Alexis Henning's body has been found," Stanton said. "That's all we can tell you right now."

Cara heard Ethan's breath catch in his throat. His hands tightened convulsively.

So Alexis was dead. That was it. She was dead.

Cara felt a hysterical urge to laugh. She bit the inside of her cheek, hard. Alexis was *dead*. The force of what that meant suddenly hit her full on, and her hands grew cold and slack on the chains. She could feel herself toppling forward slowly toward the ground.

Someone grabbed her shoulder. She looked up into Fitzgerald's impassive face. "All right, Miss Lange?"

Cara nodded. She knew her face was paper white. Ethan was standing between the two cops now. He looked somehow smaller, shrunken, next to them. As if he were already fading away from her. "Ethan," she whispered.

He didn't respond. One of the cops grasped his arm above the elbow and turned him toward the cruiser.

Frozen to the swing, Cara watched, the cold rubber strap pressing into her, as Ethan climbed into the back of the car and then was gone.

Chapter 26

CARA RAN STUMBLING THROUGH THE SILENT STREETS. *Ethan's gone, Alexis is dead,* her mind droned over and over. Her chest heaved. Tears and snot dripped from her nose.

She burst through the front door of the house. "Zoe!" she shouted into the gloom. Her breath sobbed in and out of her lungs. She clenched her fists. "Zoe!" she screamed again. Her voice broke.

Zoe appeared at the top of the stairs. She'd changed out of the red lace nightgown and discarded Samson, God knows where. Now she was wearing jeans and a black turtleneck. She glided down the steps toward Cara. As she drew closer, Cara could see that she'd wiped the makeup from her face. It was perfectly bare and shone with cleanliness. Her hair looked freshly washed, hanging in a silken curtain on either side of her face. In spite of herself, Cara caught her breath. Zoe was as beautiful as the first day she'd arrived, sitting at the edge of Cara's bed. The fetid smell was gone, Cara realized too. As if it had never existed.

Only a faint scent of lavender soap wafted toward Cara.

"Yes?" Zoe smiled pleasantly, as if Cara were an unexpected visitor.

For a moment, Cara was thrown off-balance. She stood uncertainly as Zoe watched her, still smiling gently. "The police came and took Ethan away," she finally said. The words sounded hollow.

"Oh?" Zoe nodded and raised her eyebrows, as if Cara had just told her she'd always hated cantaloupe. "That's too bad."

Cara blinked. "What?" Then she recovered. "Yes, it is too bad." She stepped closer to her friend, the rage building in her chest again. "Alexis is dead, Zoe! She's dead, and Ethan is being investigated." She leaned in. "I know you did something to her. I know it!" Her voice rose to a hysterical scream.

"Yes." Zoe smiled and nodded, still with that pleasant, polite smile on her lips.

Cara stopped. "Did you say 'yes'?"

"Yes." Zoe nodded. "I killed the bitch. And I stuffed her body in the rafters of that old barn you love so much." She smiled pleasantly and sat down on a straight chair in the foyer, crossing her legs daintily. She stroked the upholstered cloth arm of the chair with her fingertips. "Took awhile, too. The killing, I mean. I'd forgotten how long it takes to strangle someone," she said almost dreamily.

Cara's breath caught in her throat. Zoe had killed Alexis. And it wasn't the first time she'd strangled someone. Zoe's own words echoed hauntingly in Cara's head. *I did something bad, Cara. But it's not anything worse than what he did to me.*

Zoe stared off into the distance for a minute, then seemed

210

to snap back to reality. "Anyhow, once she was dead, it was pretty easy to drag her out to the woods. Getting her up into the rafters, now *that* was a chore." She laughed, a bright, happy laugh. "Dead weight, Cara. Have you ever felt true dead weight?"

Numbly, Cara shook her head. Her eyes were locked on Zoe's sweet, angelic face.

"Well, let me tell you, I could have used a hand." Zoe's voice changed. "Where were you, Cara?"

Cara stared at her, not sure she'd heard her right. "What do you mean? I was with Ethan that night." Her lips were numb.

"Yeah, that's right." Zoe pinched the chair arm again, harder this time. "Out there, having fun with your new boy-friend. While I was out in the cold, shoving your worst enemy into the rafters. She got stuck halfway up, did you know that, Cara? She got stuck and almost fell all the way down to the floor."

"Stop," Cara whispered. Her stomach churned. An image of Alexis's bright blond hair hanging down from the rafters flashed into her mind. A single white arm, dangling, the finger-tips pointing at the floor. That day in the barn. The day after the party. The flash of white in the corner. Alexis had been there, hanging right above Cara's very head, this entire time.

"Why, Cara? Why should I stop?" Zoe's voice grew a little louder. "Why? I did it all for you. Everything's been for you. All this time. And have you appreciated what I've done? First, that fat bitch Sydney—"

Cara backed away, her hands pressed to her mouth. "Sydney? You mean she didn't . . . drown?" Her voice rose to a gaspy shriek. She stumbled over a pair of shoes on the floor, and almost fell.

"Then Alexis. I choked them—I thought that'd be fitting. A little payback for the girls who called you Choker. Besides, how could you be with Ethan with Alexis in the way? All for you, sweetheart, all for you." Zoe suddenly ripped the arm of the chair out from the base savagely.

Cara jumped. Zoe stood up and walked toward her slowly. Her violet eyes blazed in her paper-white face. "And have you appreciated it? Have you said 'Thank you, Zoe' just once? No." She stopped an inch from Cara's face. "*'When are you leaving, Zoe?'*" She mimicked Cara's voice. "That's all I get. Running around with Ethan, leaving me alone. *You owe me*, Cara. *You owe me*." She was almost screaming.

Cara took another step back. She felt something solid behind her. The door. She pressed herself against it. "Sydney, too? You killed both of them? Zoe, you have to tell someone," she whispered. "The police. You have to tell the police."

Zoe snorted. "Sure, Cara. I'll just waltz in there: 'Hi, folks. Let that nice boy go. I'm your murderer—right here.'" She pointed to her chest, then flipped her hand at Cara dismissively. "You always did live in a dream world, Cara. Maybe it's time to wake up."

In her mind, Cara saw Ethan sitting at a metal table in a harshly lit little room. Two cops were standing over him, shouting. His face was streaked with tears. She shook her head. "No, Zoe."

Zoe turned around, and Cara shrank back at the venom in her face. "What did you say?" Zoe asked. Her voice was dangerously quiet.

Cara trembled, but she forced herself to go on. "If you won't go to the police, I will. I'll tell them everything." Her voice barely rose above a whisper. She pressed her palms to the door behind her. It felt cool to the touch.

Zoe studied Cara's face, smiling a little. Then she shook her head. "You left me back with my stepfather, Cara. You were the only one who knew how bad it was, *and you left me behind to rot.* So you won't go to the police. You can't. You owe me, Cara."

"I didn't ask for this!" Cara suddenly screamed. She felt something loosen and burst inside of her. "I didn't ask you for any of this! I don't want it. I don't want it." She broke off suddenly, and feeling behind her with one hand, shakily lowered herself onto the straight chair. She bent over and hugged her chest to her knees, pressing her face into her jeans.

"We're in this together, Cara. And you know it." Zoe wrenched open the door, yanking it so hard, it smashed the plaster of the wall behind it. She flew down the steps, her black hair fanning out behind her like a pair of wings, and fled into the dimming afternoon light. Cara hugged her chilly upper arms, the only comfort left to her, and watched her go.

Chapter 27

THE NIGHT FELL SLOWLY. SHADOWS GATHERED IN the corner of the kitchen, where Cara sat at the table, the picture of her and Zoe on the bike before her. The light grew dimmer, and the gray squares of the windows gradually grew black.

Zoe killed Alexis. She killed Alexis and stuffed her body in the rafters of the barn. Cara had a sudden urge to get up and go down to the barn, even though she knew the body was gone. Just to see the space with her own eyes. But a small, sane part of her mind told her to stay. Zoe was out there somewhere. And she was angry.

Vaguely, Cara thought she should get up and turn the lights on, but something held her in her seat. Some thought that if Zoe came back, she'd be harder to find in the dark.

The last light was gone from the sky now. The refrigerator and stove were just squatting hulks in the dark kitchen. The clock on the wall ticked inexorably. That was the only sound. Cara sat still. She didn't move a finger. She barely breathed. If she held perfectly still, if she didn't budge one inch, then Zoe couldn't find her.

Suddenly, the cell phone at her elbow exploded. Cara bit back the scream at her lips so hard she drew blood. Her heart hammering, she stared at the tiny glowing screen. It was Mom. Her hand was shaking so hard she fumbled the phone, dropping it, before she managed to get the case open.

"Honey?" Her mother's voice seemed to come from another planet.

"Hi, Mom," Cara whispered. She wiped at the trickle of blood running down her chin from her bitten lip.

"How's everything, honey? Are you okay?"

Cara could hear the chatter of conversation in the background. She pictured her parents in her grandmother's brightly lit living room, the TV on as usual. Grandpa Lorin in his recliner, the remains of dinner spread on the table behind them. She stared into the darkness.

"Mom, there's something wrong here," she whispered. "I need help."

"What is it, Cara?" Her mother sounded startled. "Honey, what is it?"

"It's Zoe. She's back, and she's done something awful." She waited, breathing. She felt lighter. It would be okay now. At least she wasn't alone. Her parents would help her figure out what to do.

"Zoe? Oh, no. No, Cara." Her mother's voice was stricken. "Cara, tell me what's happened. What's the awful thing? Cara? Cara?" Cara felt a strong urge to close her eyes. She needed dark, just for a minute. From behind her eyelids, she heard a scrabbling, scratching sound, and suddenly her mother's voice was cut off.

"Mom?"

But the phone was dead. Cara took it away from her ear and stared at it in her hand. It felt too light all of a sudden. There was something on the table in front of her. The battery. She turned the phone over. The back gaped open.

Cara stared at it. Then the house phone exploded from the kitchen corner. Cara jumped. But she couldn't get out of her seat. Zoe might find her. The phone rang and rang, but before she could answer it, she heard the soft tap of footsteps. They were coming from the front porch. Her breath stopped. Maybe it was just a branch, scraping against the porch. But there weren't any trees around the house. She sat upright, listening.

Scritch. Scritch. Now it sounded as if someone was scratching their nails against the door. *Scritch.* Cara's breath caught in her throat. She pictured Zoe, crouched like a cat on the front porch, scratching her fingernails to be let in. With a sense of inevitable dread, Cara heard the front door latch creak open. Zoe was here. Her footsteps were coming across the foyer. She was in the living room now. Now she was across the living room. Now she was in the kitchen.

A figure appeared in the doorway. Cara screamed. She screamed and screamed as hands grasped her shoulders. Someone was shouting her name. Zoe was shouting her name just before she wrapped her hands around Cara's neck to strangle her, like she'd strangled Sydney and Alexis.

"Cara! Cara!" It wasn't Zoe's voice. It was a man's voice. The hands on her shoulders were a man's—Ethan's. Ethan was standing in front of her.

Cara collapsed in his arms, sobbing hysterically. "She was

here, Ethan," she sobbed. "Then she ran out. And I don't know where she is. I'm so scared."

"Cara, Cara." Ethan gripped her shoulders and looked down into her face. "It's okay. I'm here now. Whatever's the matter, it's okay." He wrapped his arms around her and pulled her into his chest, cradling her until her sobs slowed, then stopped. "Okay. There, that's better."

He eased her into a chair at the table and went over to the sink. Cara heard him running water, and then a warm, wet dishcloth was put in her hand. At the same time, he flicked on the overhead lights, flooding the room. Cara blinked in the sudden brightness. The ordinary kitchen was there around her, solid. She felt her panic subside. Shakily, she pressed the wet cloth to her face.

Suddenly she remembered what had happened just a few hours ago. "Ethan, you're back. What happened at the station?"

His face clouded over. He sat down at the table. "I was questioned and released." His voice had a hard edge. "Questioned in my own girlfriend's death! They were complete assholes about it, too." The edge slipped from his voice, and he suddenly buried his face in his hands. His shoulders bowed. "I'm telling you, Cara, it was awful. They kept asking me what we'd argued about, where had I gone after I dropped you off. They weren't saying they thought I did it, but I could tell that's what they were thinking. And she's dead!" His voice broke. "She's really dead. That's the worst of it. Her body . . ." He trailed off, unable to finish his sentence.

Cara stroked his back. His pain reached out like waving tendrils. "I know," she murmured. "I can't bear to think of her rotting in the barn like that." She shook her head.

Ethan raised his head. Tears had left a few wet streaks down his cheeks. "What are you talking about? How do you know that?"

Cara stared at him, frozen. His wide blue eyes stared back. Then his expression changed. His brows drew together. "What were you talking about when I came in? Who was here?"

Cara's mouth opened and shut a few times. She longed to tell him everything, but there was a block inside her, preventing her from speaking. Ethan leaned forward and laid his hand over her clenched fist resting on the table. "What's going on, Cara?" His voice was low and intense.

Cara could feel the pressure inside her build to a peak and then, under Ethan's blue gaze, release. She opened her mouth and, with a great shuddering sigh, poured out the entire awful story, starting with Zoe's appearance in her bedroom, her strange behavior, and, finally, her confession that she'd killed both Sydney and Alexis. Finally, Cara stopped talking and stared at her jeans. Her shirt had a smear of lipstick on it. Ethan sat back in his chair. He looked as if someone had hit him in the face several times.

"Cara . . . we have to go to the police," he said. He drew his arm over his brow as if trying to keep all he'd learned inside his head. "This girl is out there somewhere, and she's dangerous. We have to find her."

Cara nodded silently. She couldn't fight it anymore. Zoe would have to be found, and she'd have to confess.

The game was up.

Chapter 28

CARA PUSHED HER WAY THROUGH THE DEAD GOLDENROD in the field behind her house. Overhead, clouds scudded across an inky sky. Her flashlight bounced ahead of her like a ghostly spotlight, illuminating a branch, a patch of ground, the trees nearby. The air was cold, frosty, and her breath hung in a cloud in front of her face.

Behind her, Ethan walked carefully in her path, holding his own flashlight. Cara could hear him breathing behind her. She could tell from the rustling and crackling in his wake that Stanton and Fitzgerald were following closely behind. Their own flashlights cast powerful beams that cut into the blackness. They'd left their cruiser outside of Cara's house after she and Ethan had called the station. Cara had told them there was only one place Zoe could be.

They were nearing the barn. The evidence inside had already been removed, the cops had said, and all the necessary fingerprints taken. Cara could see the bulk of the barn up ahead through the trees. The silvery gray walls seemed almost to shimmer in the night. Cara's flashlight shone on the trunks of the trees, then bobbed over to the barn door, still draped with crime-scene tape. Her heart clenched when she saw the door was partially ajar. She turned around.

"She's here!" she hissed.

Stanton and Fitzgerald stopped immediately and fanned out, concealing themselves adroitly behind nearby bushes. Ethan stepped behind a tree. According to the plan they'd made back at Cara's house, the officers would stay outside if Zoe was in the barn. Cara would go in and try to reason with Zoe, have her come out quietly.

Cara crept up to the barn door. She stopped at the inky crack and listened. For a long moment, she heard nothing. Maybe she was wrong. Maybe Zoe had run away. Then she heard it: a soft rustling. The rustle came again. She was in there.

Cara turned around, and her eyes met Ethan's. His forehead was creased with concern. He started to come to her. Cara shook her head violently and motioned him back. *I'll be okay,* she mouthed. He reluctantly slipped behind the tree again.

Cara turned back to the door. She turned sideways and, with difficulty, slipped through the crack in the door. The interior was an impenetrable wall of blackness. Cara pressed her back against the reassuring scratchy roughness of the barn door. Then she lifted her flashlight. She gasped when it fell on Zoe's figure standing only two feet away, cold and pale in the ghostly beam.

"I was expecting you, Cara," Zoe said. She wasn't smiling. Her voice was cold and dead. "Traitor."

The word floated on the air between them.

"Zoe, it's over," Cara said. She heard the quaver in her voice and steadied it. Her heart was pounding so loud in her ears, she could barely hear anything else. She felt surprisingly dizzy for a moment, vertigo overtaking her. Against her will, she glanced up at the barn rafters, half-expecting to see Alexis's dead face staring down at her. But it was utterly black. The body had been taken away by now. With an effort, Cara dragged her gaze back to Zoe, standing in front of her. "The police are outside, Zoe," she said. "You have to come out."

"I can't believe you'd do this to your best friend." Zoe's voice cracked, and suddenly her shoulders sagged. She started weeping, openly, heartbreakingly, like a child. Her gasping sobs tore at Cara. As if in a dream, she stepped toward her friend. Zoe lifted her head, her hair hanging in her face. "I loved you," she wept. "I loved you."

Cara felt her hands come up and touch Zoe's face. "I love you, too," she whispered. "Things just went wrong somewhere."

Suddenly, Zoe grasped Cara's wrists with frightening speed. Cara gasped in horror. Zoe's face was white, her eyes blazing jewels set deep in her skull.

"It's not over," she spat. Before Cara could react, Zoe shoved her brutally. She fell to the dirt floor with a teeth-rattling jolt. Then Zoe was on her, clinging to her with her elbows and knees, like a huge, bony spider. Her face loomed above Cara, floating like the moon. Cara turned her head from side to side, straining her limbs to get free, but Zoe was dead weight on top of her. Dead weight. *Have you ever really felt dead weight?*

Cara opened her mouth and screamed with all her strength.

Her voice cracked, and her throat burned, but she screamed again. The sound was muffled in the vastness of the barn, and she felt a flash of the same desperation as the day she'd choked—that no one was going to hear her. There was no one to help.

But behind her, she heard a rumbling like thunder and understood that Ethan was there, tugging open the doors. "Cara!" she heard him shout. Zoe suddenly released her, jumping to her feet, and Cara pushed herself to her knees, just as Stanton and Fitzgerald ran to her side. Ethan clutched her arm.

"You stupid bitch," Zoe spat. Her face was contorted in a mask of rage. "You think you're safe. But you're wrong— you're so wrong."

She turned as if to run toward the door.

"Get her!" Cara screamed. "Ethan! Get her!" She tried to run after Zoe, but she tripped, falling heavily to the floor again. She pushed herself up on her hands and knees. "She's getting away!" She pointed. Zoe slipped through the doors. But no one moved. Stanton and Fitzgerald just stood like statues, staring at her. All the color was gone from Ethan's face. He reached down and pulled Cara to her feet.

"Ethan," she sobbed again. "Please, she's getting away."

"Cara!" Ethan shouted. "There's no one there." His face was furrowed with confusion. "There's no one there," he repeated, more quietly.

Stanton and Fitzgerald lowered their arms. Cara saw them glance at each other. All three pairs of eyes fixed on Cara. She shrank back. "What? What do you mean? She attacked me! She was right there . . . you saw her . . . didn't you?" she whimpered.

Fitzgerald raised his eyebrows. He grasped Cara's arm. His fingers felt like steel bands above her elbow. "You're going to have to come with us, Cara."

Ethan gasped. "Oh, Cara, no . . ." A sudden look of realization flashed over his face, and he exhaled and sat down on the floor as if all the strength had gone out of his legs.

Cara tried to yank her arm away from Fitzgerald, but his hand only tightened. "Ethan, help me," she pleaded. "They don't understand—it was Zoe." Her breath was coming in wheezes. The tears built in her chest.

Ethan stepped toward her. Stanton put her arm out. "I'm sorry. Miss Lange, you'll have to come with us."

"Ethan!" Cara called over her shoulder as the police marched her away. "Help me!"

Chapter 29

THE INTERROGATION ROOM WAS SMALL AND DIRTY. The walls were bare cinder blocks, and the fluorescent lights overhead cast a harsh glare on everything. Cara sat at the single metal table, her head in her hands. Her parents sat on either side. Stanton and Fitzgerald stood in front of them.

"We started home as soon as Cara called," Mom was explaining. "I could tell Cara was entering a state when she said that Zoe was back. We were frantic when we were cut off. We left immediately."

Stanton made a note on the yellow pad in front of her. "What do you mean by a 'state,' Mrs. Lange?"

Her mother glanced at her father. She took a deep breath. "Cara's had psychiatric problems for a long time, officers." Her hand rhythmically stroked Cara's back as she talked. "It started when she was very small. She used to talk a lot about her imaginary friend, Zoe. All little kids have imaginary friends, but Cara's seemed somehow . . . more real. She would play a lot in the abandoned house across the street, and when she came home, she'd tell me all the things she and Zoe had been doing there. She called it 'Zoe's house.'"

Mom took a breath before she went on. "A lot of things would go wrong in our house: things breaking, items disappearing. And Cara always insisted it was Zoe. She even told me it was Zoe when I found a paring knife in her room. That was our first inkling something wasn't . . . right with Cara."

Cara stared into the dark cave of her arms. She could hear one of them scribbling on a pad.

Dad cleared his throat. "It, ah, really became clear to us that something needed to be done when a neighbor saw Cara poisoning a dog that lived on our block when Cara was in the fifth grade. The dog had bitten her earlier in the week." His mouth was a grim line. "Whenever Cara would have a hard time, she'd start talking about Zoe again. Finally, after the dog incident, we thought she might do better with a change of environment. That's when we moved here."

Cara raised her head. Her face was stiff with dried tears. "It was Zoe's idea!" she cried. "She was the one who stole the poison."

"Cara, Cara." Mom patted her on the shoulder. She turned to Stanton, who wore a neutral expression. "I don't want you to think we're negligent, officer. Cara actually did quite well after we moved. We had her see an excellent psychiatrist, Dr. Robert Samuels, and she was given some new medication that seemed to clear up the delusions. But . . . I think things have been hard for Cara at school this year, and she must have stopped taking her medication."

Stanton stopped writing and looked up. "And how do you know that, Mrs. Lange?"

Her mother hesitated and glanced at her father, who nodded. She pulled a little silk pouch out of her purse.

"Give me that!" Cara grabbed at it. Fitzgerald stepped forward half a foot. Cara subsided back into her chair. Her mother continued.

"I found about three weeks' worth of pills in Cara's jewelry box when we arrived home." She emptied the pouch onto the table. Little blue pills ran bouncing off the edges and rolled into the grimy corners of the room.

"It was all Zoe's fault! She did everything. She begged me to hide her!" Cara shouted. She swiped her hand across the table, scattering the few pills that remained. One rolled into Stanton's lap. Stanton stared at it dispassionately for a moment before plucking it out of her lap between thumb and forefinger and depositing it on the table.

"Honey, Zoe isn't real. She's in your head." Her mother placed a hand on top of hers and squeezed.

Cara jerked her hand away. Her mother's touch was irritatingly soft. "How can you say she's not real, Mom, when she's been living in my room for the last few weeks?" She stared defiantly at her parents, waiting for their look of surprise, then anger. But instead, all she saw was sadness on their faces. Her father glanced significantly at the officers. Stanton laid down her pen.

Just then, the radio sitting on the table crackled. Fitzgerald brought it up to his ear and listened attentively. Cara strained to make out the voice on the other end, but she couldn't. "Got it," Fitzgerald said. He slid the radio onto his belt. "They ran the name," he said to Stanton. "There's no Zoe Davis in the system. Only one set of prints in the barn. All matching those

229

of Cara Lange. And the pearl found in Cara's pocket matches too. Alexis Henning's necklace."

Stanton nodded and pushed her metal chair back with a screech. She stood up. "Mr. Lange, Mrs. Lange, we need to inform you also that the finger marks found on Alexis Henning's neck correspond to similar marks on Sydney Powers," she said. "We didn't have conclusive evidence before, just suspicions. In such cases, we prefer not to share those details with the public. But with this new evidence, Sydney's cause of death is being changed from accidental drowning to suspected homicide."

Cara's parents gasped. Mom pressed her hand to her mouth. Cara stood up, knocking her chair over. Stanton and Fitzgerald snapped to attention, their hands going to their belts.

"You've always hated Zoe!" Cara shouted. Her voice sounded muffled in the tiny room. "You thought her family wasn't good enough. But just because you hate her doesn't mean you can pretend she doesn't exist. I have proof! I have this picture right here." From her pocket, she pulled the wrinkled photo of Zoe and her and thrust it into their faces.

But no one moved. The cops glanced at each other. Stanton raised her eyebrows at Fitzgerald. Mom and Dad sat silently, their heads bowed. Cara dropped her arms. The picture fluttered from her slack grasp and fell to the dirty linoleum. Alone on the bicycle, the little girl in the photo grinned out at them all.

Epilogue

OPRAH WAS INTERVIEWING A CHEF. HE WAS EXPLAINING why he loved scallions so much. Cara sighed and shifted on the rough, nubbly couch cushion. The couch in the common room gave her a rash on her legs. "Oprah, let me tell you how important it is to get your scallions fresh," the chef said on the screen. Cara bared her teeth at him and leaned over to grab the economy-size Vaseline from the coffee table in front of her. Lifting each leg, she methodically smeared the grease all up and down the red, abraded streaks on the undersides of her legs.

Besides the faded brown couch she was sitting on, the only other furniture in the common room was a sagging orange love seat and a few spindly folding chairs, all facing the ancient TV. Cara was the only one here. Everyone else was at Physical Activity, but Cara was exempt because she ran on a treadmill each morning. They said the structure was good for her.

Next door, she could hear Wanda wailing. They must be trying to get her dressed again. She'd been wandering down the halls lately with only her pajama top on, insisting she was late for an appointment with Jesus.

"Back after this." Oprah's face faded, replaced by the hard-faced weather woman.

"It's going to be a nasty day out there," she chirped. "Sleet expected through tomorrow, so remember your mittens!"

Cara's gaze wandered to the single window. The glass was green-tinted and double thick, reinforced with wire mesh. She certainly wouldn't be out in the sleet today.

Oprah was introducing a makeup artist when Phyllis bustled in through the open door. "Meds!" the nurse caroled. Today her scrubs had little teddy bears scattered all over them. Cara clicked off Oprah.

"How are you today, Miss Cara?" Phyllis asked. She drew back the curtains a little more, allowing in a feeble trickle of light. "Feeling a little more cheerful?"

Cara mustered up the obligatory smile. "Oh sure," she said. She held out her hand, and Phyllis deposited three pills onto her palm. Blue, white, and pink. Cara put them on her tongue. Phyllis put a paper cup of water in her hand, and Cara took it. She propped her feet on the coffee table and stared at the black TV screen while the nurse, sensing her mood, turned toward the door. "Art therapy at one," she said over her shoulder. With a huge effort, Cara turned her head and nodded. She smiled again, and Phyllis, apparently satisfied, smiled back and retreated.

Cara picked up the remote again when Phyllis's rubber-soled footsteps squeaked back down the hall toward the common room. She popped her head in the door. "Aren't you going to eat something?"

Cara looked at the wall clock. Noon. She ate lunch at this time every day, even though she was never hungry. Sometimes she talked to the other patients, but on days when everyone was at Physical Activity, she ate alone, which she preferred anyway. She heaved herself up from the couch. "Okay."

Phyllis led Cara down the hall to the small linoleum-floored room that served as the cafeteria. She left Cara at the door and went into the nurses' station next door, to mark charts at the desk. Cara, her gaze downcast, chose a chair and sat. She stared down at the sad plate of peas and chicken Phyllis had set out for her.

"Careful not to choke," a familiar, gravelly voice said.

Cara's breath stopped. She looked up to see violet eyes and a swath of shiny jet-black hair.

"Listen, I'm really sorry about the way everything turned out," Zoe went on, taking the seat across from Cara in the empty room. "But look on the bright side." A smile curled across her perfect pink lips. "Now we have plenty of time to catch up."